L LIE

By the same author in PAN Books

HAMMERHEAD
SHAMELADY
SERGEANT DEATH (*Once in a Lifetime*)

LET SLEEPING GIRLS LIE

JAMES MAYO

UNABRIDGED

PAN BOOKS LTD · LONDON

First published 1965 by William Heinemann Ltd.
This edition published 1967 by Pan Books Ltd.,
33 Tothill Street, London, S.W.1

ISBN 0 330 10602 3

2nd Printing 1968
3rd Printing 1969
4th Printing 1970

Printed in Great Britain by Richard Clay (The Chaucer Press), Ltd.,
Bungay, Suffolk

unhook the bra, she swayed and nearly fell. Her hand wrenched at a shoulder-strap, snapped it. She pulled the bra off. The firm uptilted breasts did not sag. She got out of her pants. Then again a bubble of laughter began to rise from deep inside her.

'Oh God.' She tried to choke it down. She crushed her hands over her nude breasts. A look of terror came into her eyes while the irrepressible laughter welled up and took possession of her.

She staggered across the room, knocked over a standard lamp. She fumbled open a suitcase, then fell upsetting the contents over the floor. She got to her knees, racked with laughter, then to her feet, reeled towards the bed. Blindly her palm pressed all the bell-pushes at once. A vase of flowers on the night table overturned. Trying to reach the spilled belongings to cover herself, she staggered again, clasped the curtains and brought them down with a crash.

She lay on her back, one knee bent, one hand vainly raised to her mouth. Her breasts quivered; violent tremors shook her at intervals. One stocking had torn away from the narrow suspender belt round her hips. She rolled her head from side to side.

Somebody knocked on the door. She tried to raise herself but fell back. The door opened and the chambermaid and floor waiter came in. The man gave a glance, retreated. But the maid called to him to stay outside. She tried to lift the girl, muttering, 'Pauvre petite, what's the matter?'

The girl made an effort to speak, spluttered and exploded with laughter again. She lay, nude, limp and beautiful on the carpet, given over to wave after wave of that tearing hilarity.

The maid picked a dress from the clothes scattered on the floor, flung it over her and called the waiter in. Together they lifted her. The girl's arm brushed off the covering. The young waiter reddened. They put her into the bed.

'Call Monsieur Edouard,' the maid said.

Footsteps hurried down the corridor and came back with others. More came. There were many hurrying feet – the manager's, a nurse's, the director's and at last a doctor's. The girl's laughter came faintly through from the room. Passing guests glanced at each other in amusement, catching the infectious hilarity and smiling.

'Well! *Somebody's* having a good time,' said a woman, lighting a rose-tipped cigarette.

The girl was inert except for giggles which shook her from time to time. The doctor sat beside her and began talking to her gently and softly. He was Dr Hedegaard, a celebrated Danish physician who was staying in the hotel. His hand sought hers, taking her pulse. The girl's eyes were shut. But as he spoke quietly to her, her giggles strengthened and became louder and louder. She arched her back as the paroxysm swept over her. Her hands moved convulsively. She seemed to be fighting demons. Trembling shook her. Her inordinate laughter filled the room.

The hotel group stood watching motionless and white-faced. The doctor rose and came over to the director standing apart. Their mouths moved but everything seemed to be silent except for the girl's laughter. In fact the director said, 'Has she lost her mind?'

'I do not know,' the doctor said.

'Hysteria?'

'No.'

'But, Doctor, something must be done for her. I have known her since she was a child. I know her parents. They are dear friends.'

The doctor shrugged. 'There is ... I hesitate to make a guess with so little examination. But there is a disease called *kuru*. It is known as laughing death.'

'Laughing death?' The director's eyes were fixed on him.

'It is obscure and terrible. It is known in New Guinea. Those who have it laugh themselves to death.'

Slowly they turned. The laughter had stopped. The

doctor stepped to the bedside, took her wrist and bent over the girl. He lifted his head and looked at the others.

He let her arm drop.

CHAPTER TWO

THE STONE portal beside the headquarters of ICC, the mighty International Chemicals Corporation, looked a sheer anachronism. Its Doric pillars, the massive pediment, seemed to be symbols of something once great which had now passed away. The contrast between it and the modern ICC block which shouldered it was absurd. Visitors who did not know the City well and were seeking ICC, sometimes looked up at that austere, blackened and nameless entrance, wondered fleetingly if this could be it. But the next second they were sure it wasn't and passed on.

Only some two dozen men daily went in under the high stone portal. They were men whose power was unquestioned from the City of London to distant places of the world. They were the senior directors of ICC and the building they had unanimously preserved and from which they ruled the vast ICC complex, stood for them and for the City of London alike, for the permanence of ICC's power.

That morning, Hood leaned forward in his taxi and said, 'This is it.' The taxi pulled up.

'No number,' the taximan said, looking up unfavourably at the entrance.

'I'm always telling them,' Hood said with a smile.

'What is it, some club?'

'Old-style Turkish bath.'

'Thought so. Thank you, sir. Much obliged.'

Hood went up the step. To a hasty passer-by, he was indistinguishable from the very few other men who entered the building except that he was younger and wore a felt hat with a short brim instead of the uniform bowler. Moreover, he carried no paper or umbrella, which might have seemed suspicious to some. But his dark blue two-piece suit with the faint red stripe, his tie and black shoes, looked of a pattern with several million worn by the City men around him. Hood, who was a thousand miles from a conformist, believed in conforming on these occasions.

At the top of the steps, the door was heaved open by a commissionaire with a VC's ribbon on his chest.

'Good morning, Mr Hood.' The commissionaire saluted.

'Good morning, Jackson.'

The entrance was suddenly cool after the street outside. Hood went up more steps with white pipe-clayed edges and through a padded door where a porter in the Corporation's bottle-green livery, gold chain and cocked hat took his trilby.

'Good morning, Mr Hood.'

'How are you, Barfoot?'

Beyond a farther door, in glass, Hood stepped into the ceremonial hall lighted from the high cupola above – if it could be called lighted. There was a sort of sanctified gloom. It was like a small cathedral to the millions and the might that had been generated there, removed from the rest of the world. His heels rang on the marble flooring; but that was the only sound except the faint skittering of teleprinters somewhere, like commercial prayers.

'By God, it gets gloomier,' Hood thought. 'I must tell Jack to get it fixed up with a few spots.'

White marble busts loomed in corners. Varnished portraits and monstrous mercantile scenes gleamed down on him. His feet struck carpet, thick, red and muffling. Great mahogany banisters wound glinting up and there were more portraits on the stairs. Hood went on the small lift which, as a concession to human frailty, the Board had had put in. He tried to slam the door; but it couldn't be slammed. It twitched noiselessly to on an arm. He thumbed the button to the third floor.

At the top a liveried porter greeted him. 'Would you come along, sir? Miss Page is waiting.' They had rung up from the front door. Hood reflected again that it was harder to get into this sanctum, or at least go unaccompanied, than plenty of other places he knew where the security was supposed to be absolute. They went past red-varnished doors. There were two or three Sheraton chairs in coral-stained leather, a delicate writing-desk with a piece of Meissen on it. Hood glanced at the Meissen affectionately and grinned. He had given it to ICC himself. It was a Kaendler harlequin and he had presented it after a particularly risky assignment for ICC because, he said, it would help him get over the effect of the entrance whenever he had to call. He couldn't imagine it was there habitually. The austerity wouldn't stand it. Somebody had put it out for him now.

Miss Page was a pleasant impassive woman in her mid-thirties. After their greetings, Hood said, 'Is the Chairman in, Hilary?'

'Yes, but he's just got a call from Downing Street. He asked would you wait.'

'All right. How is he?'

She had opened the door to Lord Claymore's outer office. She coughed. 'Disturbed, I think. But he hasn't told me what about.' She associated Hood with trouble and therefore, with deadly feminine logic, didn't entirely approve of him. She shut the door behind him.

Hood moved round the big oval room with its massive pieces of furniture and marble columns. Lately there had been an effort to lighten the overpowering effect. He lit a cigarette. He stood at the window gazing out on to the windows, walls and roofs of the City.

ICC was one of the consortium of financial and industrial powers known as 'The Circle' for whom Hood worked as inside man and confidential agent. The Circle was a highly exclusive group whose existence was legendary in the City of London, yet could never be confirmed by those who were outside it. Twenty tycoons, a dozen great corporations in Britain would have given a million to charity for membership. But membership of The Circle was not something they could buy.

It was made up of ten of the dominant financial and industrial powers of England. Periodically there were rumblings in the City and in the papers; questions were asked in Parliament and the Unions about its existence and its activities. In the early days, after a blazing row at question time, the Prime Minister had had a private talk with the Leader of the Opposition and the Liberals and briefed them on The Circle's role as an adjunct of national security. There had been understanding; and only those who did not know the facts now tried to start rows.

The Prime Minister had not thought fit to tell the two other leaders that Charles Hood, The Circle's undercover man, also happened to be a member of HM secret service* by which he was seconded when necessary. But in this conversation in his private room at the Commons, he made enough clear to them for them perhaps to guess it. And they were all agreed that the defence of The Circle's affairs interlocked inextricably with the defence of Britain's wider interests and played directly upon them. A blow at The Circle in some distant place could damage British power and influence there. In the opposite sense, the Government's influence and interest was made manifest, when it was not indirectly exercised, through The Circle's activities.

The crystal doorknob turned. 'Come in, Charles. Good of you to come so quickly. I wanted to make it this afternoon and have more time, but it can't be done.' Lord Claymore, Chairman of ICC, was six feet four with piercing brown eyes and craggy eyebrows and one of the finest brains in Europe. He had succeeded young, was fifty-three and didn't look it. He held open the door to his inner office. 'How are you?' They shook hands.

'Fine,' Hood said.

The inner office was smaller and more intimate. But intimacy, Hood thought, could only ever be relative in

* See the exciting story *Hammerhead*.

that building. A couple of years before, he had amused himself trying to persuade Jack Claymore to hang a Rothko in his office. Claymore had gone as far as going to see one with him at the Marlborough; but he had immediately said: 'No, no. It won't do. Is this one of your jokes?'

'Then what about that Van Dongen over there? Believe me, it's an investment. If I had a stack of blue chips to invest, I'd buy Van Dongens.'

'Come off it. Can you imagine the President of the World Bank finding that over my desk?' They had laughed.

'Sit down, my dear fellow.' Claymore pushed forward the box of cigarettes. Hood lit one. 'Hale has told you of our trouble,' Claymore went on. 'We have these two girls – twins – with whom the best of our research is bound up, and one of them has been disappearing with frightening frequency: weekends, trips to God knows where. Alas, I have only just heard of it; but it's been going on for some time. Our security people have checked here and there – you know all this. But the girl gets away every time.'

Hood nodded.

'It's not a matter of her private life. It is far more serious.'

'She's now back, I gather?'

'Yes, the little bitch got back from her last escapade three days ago.'

Hood said, 'Is she just being indiscreet?'

Claymore looked at him. He got up, towering, walked to the window and back. There was urgency in his voice. 'Damn it, Charles, we don't know! We have found out she had an affair with young Quayle and another with Le Maître's son – disquieting people. It appears that she also went to a doubtful party at Brookdon.' He gave it the correct pronunciation: Brewdon.

Hood drew on his cigarette. He had been told Claymore was anxious. It was manifest.

Claymore said unhappily: 'You see my situation over

this, Charles? I allowed myself to approve of this entirely unorthodox system. I did more, I pressed for it. I don't conceal that. There didn't seem to be a flaw. I don't say I was wrong. I am not going back on it. But now I find myself out on a limb.'

That, Hood said to himself, was putting it mildly.

'These girls are worth a million pounds to us – more! They are probably the most valuable individual human beings alive. Do you realize that? I needn't explain to you that the research they are associated with has gone on for years – a decade. We have invested millions in it, and we, of course, also means HMG. This sort of thing, Charles, is like losing a chip off the Cullinan. Something unique is gone.'

'You don't *know* that it's gone.'

Before Claymore could answer, a soft buzzer sounded on his desk. Claymore picked up the telephone. 'Yes? ... Yes please. In exactly two minutes.' To Hood he said: 'It's Whitney. He's coming in.'

Robert Whitney was Hood's associate in his work for The Circle. Hood said: 'He just got in from New York this morning. I thought it would be convenient if he followed me here in case there was anything private you wanted to say about the girl.'

'Charles, I'm damned worried.'

'Is there any secret data that you are particularly anxious about?'

'My dear fellow, there are fifty processes I should be anxious about if I thought any one of them was leaking.' Claymore paused. Then he said emphatically: 'Is it bed or is it treason? – because that's what it would amount to.'

What did that mean? Hood saw that something unexpected had cropped up. 'Is that a hint that you want to call in MI5?'

Claymore went over to the ormolu clock. He stood watching its pendulum swing. It was a familiar stance to the City, indeed to the industrial magnates of the world. Max Beerbohm's last cartoon had been of him standing there: 'Lord Claymore making up his mind on a ticklish problem.'

Then he swung round, ferocious. 'I shan't be able to keep it from the PM, Charles, if it goes on. There is too much at stake. There are going to be extremely unpleasant consequences unless we know where we stand.'

The door opened. It was Miss Page showing in Robert Whitney.

'Hello, young fellow,' Claymore said. 'Good trip?'

'Yes, thank you, sir.' Whitney was a few inches shorter than Hood and slighter in build. But his boyish figure concealed great toughness. Hood caught Claymore's look of interrogation. He shook his head. 'He is not up in this. He has been away.'

'Have you seen the pair of girls at work, Charles?'

'No.'

Claymore stepped to the desk in one lanky stride. He took the telephone and spoke into it. When he put it down, he said: 'The two of them are in the small lab next door. We'll go and look at them. They are generally out at Isleworth. It will give Whitney a chance to see them too.'

'Excellent,' Hood said. Yet he knew that for Claymore to come himself was a sign of great anxiety. Claymore was already striding for the door. Hood was curious about what was going to happen.

Outside the office they went down the corridor to another lift and down two floors. Hale, Claymore's principal assistant who had been warned that the Chairman was coming down, was waiting with a porter. Hood and Whitney barely had time to exchange greetings with Hale; Claymore was hastening on. Hale had caught the mood and looked grim.

'What's got into the old man?' Whitney whispered to Hood.

Hood gave him an enigmatic look. 'Hold it.'

They passed through heavy steel doors. The decor abruptly changed. The turkey carpet became rubberoid floor. The fluorescent lighting gave a pale, inhuman tint to the grey glass walls. At a dip of several steps in the passageway, they were held up by the security check. They all produced passes. The guard checked the identity photographs with care and after each one said: 'Kindly stand there, sir.'

Lord Claymore was first. He stood facing a small glass screen like a television screen in the wall. He had to stoop somewhat and held his identity pass at chest height. There was a smooth whirr. 'Thank you, sir,' the guard said. This was the security photographic record of all visitors to the lab area.

Hood and Hale went next. At Whitney's turn, the guard shook his head. 'Sorry, sir. This pass is out of date.'

'I must have this gentleman with me,' Lord Claymore said.

'Very well, sir. I shall have to come along. Kindly step this way, sir.' Whitney went into the cubicle and was told to put his hands, palms down, on another glass panel. He did so; the panel glowed faintly. 'Finger and palm print. New system,' Hood said to his inquiring look.

In a moment, they were again heading down the corridor. They went through further doors and after another check, entered a narrow room. The guard stopped at the door.

'Security observation room,' Hale said quietly. 'No smoking.'

The room was lit dimly with red light and there was the faint factitious ozone freshness of air conditioning. A brighter light came from a window low down in the right-hand wall. Claymore advanced to the window. There was a row of upright leather chairs in front of it. They all sat down. The window looked down into another brightly lighted room which, from their seats, they could see perfectly.

'That is the lab and from here we observe what goes on in there,' Hale explained in a low voice. He had placed his chair behind Hood and Whitney. 'Whoever's in there can't see us. This window looks like a glazed pane to them. You know the technique?'

'Sure.'

'We have a sound relay. That switch in front of you.' Hood pressed it and there was a faint crackle as the mike became live.

The lab before them was empty. They sat with the glow of light illuminating their faces, their eyes examining details – the row of deep sinks, the glass and chrome cases and steamers, trolleys, racks of bottles and tubes and the white-slab working surfaces. There was a white table in the centre.

Hood glanced at Claymore next to him. Claymore's face was set.

Then below them, the swing doors of the lab opened and two girls came in. They were talking animatedly and laughing. Hood's eyes went fast from one to the other, then rested on the girl on the right.

She had a greenish wrapper on, meant for an overall. Her hair had been done and she had a big silver bracelet on one wrist. The wrapper was swathed and held by a tight belt and Hood guessed she did not have much on under it.

The other girl was identical. She was the same height and colouring. She wore the same thin wrapper affair and obviously had the same flair for looking smart. To Hood there was momentarily a subtle, elusive difference in her. It wasn't physical – they were too alike for that. But the emanation of personality in this girl was not quite so strong. She was charming – but slightly different. The next minute he was shaking his head: there was no difference. The two were chattering and pealing with laughter.

'Who are they?' Whitney asked.

'The Evenly twins,' Hood said.

'Okay,' Whitney grinned. 'But who are they?'

'That's their name. Twin sisters. The two Lady Evenlys. The Earl of Orme's daughters. Known as the Heavenly Twins. The one on the left, if I'm right, is Tickle and the other one's Tiara.'

Whitney gave a gasp of admiration. 'Lady Tickle

Evenly . . . and Lady Tiara Evenly..Boy!'

The two girls were standing at the central table of the laboratory. The door behind them opened again. It was a man in white overalls. He carried a pad that looked like yellowed paper. He approached the table and said something to Tickle. There was a pause. Then, as the girl began to speak in reply, Claymore's voice cut across the relay from the microphone.

'She is reciting a research formula which this member of the advanced research staff – from the red and green button he is wearing you know he is working on secret metals – has asked her for. It is probably a long and complex piece of data. He is writing it down on that wax pad.'

'Wax?'

'Yes. It will efface itself in a given time, an hour, half an hour, it depends. There will then be no further record of it – except in Lady Evenly's mind.'

'Suppose he writes it down somewhere else?'

'He is searched for writing materials and of course is closely supervised. The men in any event are trusted workers.'

'Memory?'

'With a prodigious memory, he might memorize some of these secret notations, but there would be no point. We scramble them with code items. The formula, as he is given it, contains false elements – like a code or cypher contains dud letters and figure-groups which mean nothing. They are simply put in to confuse and prevent the code – or the formula in our case – being broken. We constantly change these bogus additions to make the thing more difficult to crack. Do you follow?'

Hood nodded.

'As you know, the system was primarily introduced because we had that disastrous series of leaks eighteen months ago. Even so, we are most anxious for this highly secret data – certainly not a great concentration of it, as we are dealing with here – not to be expressed on paper in its complete form. It's as if we were a bank, a broking house, a government which wanted to avoid keeping all its secret information in one file. We have been fortunate enough to find these two young women. Besides their phenomenal memories, they have a gift.

'Their minds communicate in a unique fashion. It springs from their twinship. Doctors know of it, of course. A good deal of medical research has been done on it, especially in relation to criminals – twins who were compelled to commit criminal acts in response to their "other half".'

'Compelled?'

'Yes, compelled. Sounds fantasy but it's quite the reverse. These two girls are two parts of the same brain. When one of them recalls data, the other one can summon up things she has forgotten and, in the ordinary sense, doesn't know.'

The man in the brightly lighted lab was writing to the girl's dictation. She spoke clearly and steadily. Tiara was sitting on a chair at the other end of the room.

Claymore went on. 'The twin who is now speaking only knows half the formula or notation. She may have forgotten it before this session. Sometimes the man finds it necessary to give her a figure to start her off. The other girl knows the other half. *But she doesn't know she does. She is not normally aware of it, just as an ordinary person is not normally aware of what is in his subconscious. It will only come out when her sister makes this mysterious mental communication with her and brings it up to her consciousness.* Damned curious, isn't it? But it is the perfect security system, you see. You can't give away what, in effect, you don't know.'

Abruptly the girl stopped speaking. Bent over the table writing, the man looked up at her.

'That's all,' she said.

'Now watch the other girl,' Lord Claymore said.

The man picked up the pad and walked towards Tiara. Tiara's lovely face changed. She shut her eyes and put her hands to her forehead. She bent forward in the chair as though a blinding headache had come on. There was absolute silence. A fluorescent tube flickered once or twice. They were all staring at the girl. Hood felt an upsurge of unreasoning anger, as if the girl were in pain. He couldn't take his eyes off her. Vaguely at the edge of his field of vision he was aware of the other twin immobile at the table.

Then Tiara's shoulders loosened. She sat up. She looked at the man rather blankly and began to recite figures in a monotone.

'Now, you see, she is giving the other half,' Claymore said. 'They are a unique security file. They are like two combination locks to a vault, one does not work without the other.'

They watched while Tiara went through the long recital. As she finished, she had curiously recovered, resumed her former expression and gaiety. The man went out.

'How long do they work?' Hood asked.

'Short sessions. An hour or two.'

The girls, left alone, were chattering again. Tiara had completely recovered. Tickle took out a little Cartier case, extracted a cigarette and lit it. Then, turning away from the door and facing the invisible watchers at the window, Tiara plunged, pulled open the wrapper and began hauling her stocking tight at the thigh.

The long leg showed, high up. She found some snag at the very top on the inside and turned her leg to see. Claymore coughed and shifted in his chair. Hood was grinning.

'Boy! ...' Whitney murmured. Hale pretended not to look.

As she started on the other stocking, Tickle came over. They began making some comparison of stockings, and Tickle hitched one high up too, evidently to show the length. She pivoted on her heel to show the back.

Claymore shuffled and started to say something, but before he could do so, the girls looked over their shoulders, rearranged themselves with a flip and turned. Another man in white overalls came in.

Again they went through the ritual. Again it was Tickle who began. And once more, as Tiara bent forward searching for the scientific notations she did not know she knew, Hood was moved. It seemed to take a little longer. She seemed remote. Then she lifted her head and began.

Claymore scraped back his chair and rose. 'I must leave you.' They all got up and followed him out.

'Charles, I rely on you.' Suddenly he looked grey. His lips tightened. 'We can't afford a mishap.' Characteristically brusque, he strode off.

There was a pause. The security man was edging forward. He had a note in his hand. He said something to Hale. Hale listened and turned to Hood. 'Message for you. Your secretary rang up and said Raisely Neame can see you at noon. She wants to know if you're going, so that she can confirm it.'

Sir Raisely Neame was ICC's chief medical consultant.

'Good.' Hood looked at his watch. 'Yes, we'll go now.'

Hale led them out. At the street door the commissionaire called an ICC Daimler, a V8 Majestic Major which could do 125 miles an hour and was no hearse. They gave the address and got in. As the driver headed into the City traffic, Chuck Whitney said: 'Charles, who in God is Lord Orme and how is it I never ran into these Evenly girls before?'

'You don't remember Orme?'

'I don't.'

'He was a clever eccentric, a collector; an expert on Titian and Giorgione. Used to be a great buddy of Duveen's. The girls came out here. Then Orme married a Venezuelan oil millionairess who was a bit more eccentric than he was and she made them all live in Caracas. So the girls disappeared from London life until recently.'

'Well, it won't be long before somebody's moving in those Evenly spheres.'

'Pretty, eh?'

'My God! they're good-lookers. Hale said something about there being a very, very slight difference between them – but I couldn't see it.'

'That's the trouble, the difference,' Hood said.

'How come?'

'One of them is a nympho – but they don't know which one. Now they've realized that maybe they're both nymphos – and that's much more dangerous. ICC only discovered it after they had put them in this job. One of them keeps going off on trips and they can't find out whether she is giving away this secret material or just having affairs. Or maybe they're both going away alternately.'

'Which one do they think it is?' Whitney asked.

Hood grinned. 'Couldn't you get it?'

'Yah! Which one?'

'Tiara.'

'The Inconstant Nympho, huh?'

Hood shot him a look.

'The only nympho I knew was an algebra teacher and she wore brogues,' Whitney said.

'These two suddenly confuse everybody by changing their hair-dos and switching rinses. One of them has a blonde rinse one day and the day after the other uses it and so forth. Even without make-up they're practically interchangeable.'

'So the only way of knowing which is which is to make a pass?'

'Not the only way. Maybe they're *both*.'

'But if one can't work without the other, how can she give the data away?' Whitney said. 'That's the whole idea, isn't it? If Tiara doesn't take her sister along when she goes off for a weekend in bed, there can't be any risk.'

'Not so simple. A lot of this secret material is there for whoever can find it. It exists in its own right. ICC have found it first. It's their discovery, their breakthrough that's secret and important. Of course, other data is much more complex and developed. But if you get a start, maybe you can go on from there. It's like getting a very, very difficult cypher handed to you with a clue. Maybe you can crack it. Anyway, you certainly get a new direction for research – and maybe that means a breakthrough. Besides, somebody may *already* have half the data – and need only the other half to complete.'

'What's the material?'

'They're producing metals and compounds for Harwell and stuff on lasers for the defence staff. It's way out beyond anything else so far. There is also something on non-absorbent mirrors which is a new thing and a line that has to do with the Newton Project.'

'Newton Project?'

'That's the advanced study into countering gravity that the National Physical Laboratory is on; very hush.'

'Whew! And those two girls with this stuff? It's dynamite.'

'It is; but they're clever.'

The car nosed out of the swirl at the Mansion House and headed up Cheapside. An *Evening News* bill said: POP SINGER IN BOX. A car backfired and there was a sudden swoop of pigeons. A man selling fruit from a barrow wore a Lock hat and suède shoes.

'Do you understand this communication thing?' Whitney asked.

'That's what we're going to see Neame about. He's the big medical cheese on this and I know ICC consulted him about those girls.'

They pulled up in Welbeck Street and got out.

Sir Raisely Neame was large; a comfortable belly in striped trousers and curly black hair going grey. His teeth looked larger than ordinary human size and his manner was cordial. They got through the preliminaries and Hood asked his question about the Evenly girls.

'Mind if I walk?' Neame exposed his great block of teeth. 'Can't do it with patients. Only exercise I get.' He started trudging up and down the room.

'They're very remarkable girls, aren't they? They're what you call concordant monozygotic twins. That means they come from the same single egg. Mostly it's one person per egg. With monozygotics, two people from one egg. Clear?'

They nodded.

'Ordinary twins, the ones that come from two separate eggs, are not more alike than any brothers or sisters they happen to have. Sometimes they turn out to be widely different from each other. But monozygotic twins, especially concordant ones, are so closely alike that their mothers can barely tell them apart. They have the same gestures, the same writing. They smell the same. If you examined those girls' fingerprints, even subcutaneous prints, you'd get two right hands more alike than the right and left hand of the same girl.

'Monozygotic twins fall sick from the same things. Or they stay free of them when their brothers and sisters (who may be ordinary twins) fall sick. They even fall sick at the same *time*. But the great thing is, as the Evenly girls show so well, that monozygotic twins are not merely alike physically but mentally too. They have the same mental processes. You find they have the same tastes, the same attitude about religion, money, children, travel, business — '

'Sex?'

'Yes, though not necessarily to exactly the same degree. Even concordant monozygotic twins – the supreme degree of likeness – don't show the same intensity in their attitude to everything under the sun. There can be differences in mental make-up, a mental speeding-up in one more than the other – but it is usually small. You may have one twin who is livelier, more restless, more extroverted than the other. Similarly, there *could* be a different emphasis on sex.'

'But only emphasis?'

'Yes.' Neame paused in the bay window, finger in waistcoat pocket. For a second or two his eye followed a postman going down the street. He turned back.

'There have been remarkable tests with criminal twins, you know. Professor Johannes Lange,* the great Bavarian doctor, did a lot of work on them before the war

* See his masterpiece of research, a medical classic: *Verbrechen als Schicksal. Studien an Kriminellen Zwillingen*, Leipzig, 1929.

and there have been others. They found, for instance, that monozygotic twins among criminals behave almost identically. One twin commits a crime in, say, January; the other twin, maybe hundreds of miles away, commits a crime in January or June – *but commits it.* They behave like one person. The thing is communicated. It is just a question of how long the communication takes.

'There was one experiment when they carefully separated all the true monozygotics in jail then or earlier and made a close study of their records. The result was amazing. Ordinary twins turned out to have nothing like the same similarity in behaviour. The doctors found only about ten per cent of ordinary twins behaving identically in crime. But with monozygotics, nearly eighty per cent of them had identical patterns of crime.'

'But it's merely a lapse in one of them then, a temporary state?'

'Not a bit. And it's not accident or coincidence, nothing like that. You get monozygotic twins repeating the same pattern of theft for twenty-five years and more. If you put the records side by side and find a period when there is a break with one twin, you find a break with the other. For instance, if one twin didn't steal anything for twelve months, the other one didn't either. This happened when one twin was jailed and the other wasn't for the time being. On the other hand, *nothing seems able to check the connection – the communication – being made if one twin starts it.* If one twin is in jail and keeps complaining about prison conditions, the other one, who is free, will start complaining about something analogous. If one starts fighting, the other outside – or inside – will soon be fighting too.'

'So they are victims of fate?' Hood said. 'They can't help it?'

Neame stopped walking. He looked out of the window for a minute, then back. 'That's a difficult question, Mr Hood. It could be said that *one* of the twins is, at all events, since it can't resist the urge it feels in the other. And if twins of a monozygotic pair interact on each other, then both are victims. That is where the talents of these two young women come in. Their faculty of communication is simply an extension of their ordinary behaviour pattern. They can't help it, as you put it, Mr Hood. They are merely doing mentally the same sort of thing they are compelled to do physically.'

'Suppose they were criminals – or induced to become criminals?'

'If one were a criminal, I am convinced that they would both be criminals. They could not help it. What small differences they have, apart possibly from sex emphasis, would not affect the other important aspects of their lives.'

'Putting it inexpertly, Sir Raisely, if one girl were to go seriously wrong – this is pure hypothesis – the other wouldn't be able to help going the same way?'

'She would find it impossible to resist the innate urge to.'

'And that innate urge would work in both directions?'

'In both directions, Mr Hood.'

'Thank you.' They got up to go.

Hood knew why Lord Claymore had looked grey.

CHAPTER THREE

THE STEEL GREY Citroën DS crested the rise and went like a low grey shimmer down the long stretch ahead.

Damn, damn, damn. Hood cursed steadily. He flicked a glance at the dashboard. His eyes photographed the dials, lifted back to the road. Speed 140; roughly 87 miles an hour. Oil okay. Time 1.20 pm. The car was a shade off-balance; too much air in the back off-side tyre.

The girl had fooled them again. How it had been done they didn't yet know. There had been no time to find out – and he had been tipped off too late.

He could see the turquoise 4½ litre 'R' type Bentley Continental coupé well ahead. No doubt of it, the girl could drive! She was drawing away again, the little bitch. Hood shut the last crack of open window, squeezed the DS for more. The needle flicked to 89.

Hood sat tense. He was experiencing the state of extreme awareness known to racing drivers, when every faculty of the body responds with great precision and life is lived, as it were, with the fingertips.

The road ran straight as an arrow for as far as he could see. It was lined with tall trees. Fields spread on either side. The strong sun through the leaves dappled the surface of the road. There was no distraction for the eye. It was an area meant for speed.

Grim amusement showed in Hood's dark grey eyes. He had been chasing the girl in the turquoise Bentley along the N10 since Bordeaux. Now they were almost halfway along the long monotonous stretch from Angoulême to Poitiers and she was giving the Bentley the gun. As it was, he thought, they were hitting it too damn fast.

A ten-ton lorry was moving erratically on the road ahead. The Bentley sailed past without a pause. The word 'BYRRH' on the lorry's blue stern enlarged at him at high speed. Without warning, the lorry swung over to the crown of the road. Hood reacted smoothly, eased out, jumped it. The Bentley was over the crest of a rise. When he topped it, he had the impression that she had increased her lead. The long stretch ahead was empty. The next moment, he saw that she was pulling away. She was doing 100.

Hood sat slightly more upright. His lips tightened as he tried to coax more speed out of the Citroën. If there were curves, the DS would stand to gain ground. But on this long straight stretch the girl had great advantage.

She was drawing off. A couple of cars came by from the other direction, passing in thuds of wind. The DS was rock-steady. It sat on the road as if it were pressed into it.

They passed Mansle.

Then, a mile on, a Shell trailer appeared coming towards them. Ahead to the right, Hood saw an ancient saloon approaching along a secondary road. It was not far beyond the Bentley and bucking along fairly fast. Hood winced mentally as he saw what was going to happen, and cut speed. As he expected, the saloon reached the main road and, ignoring the 'Halt' sign, swung wide out on it, turning right too – just as the Shell trailer reached the spot.

Hood stopped breathing. The Bentley shot through the gap between the trailer and the swinging saloon with ten inches' clearance. It was done without a flinch.

Hood gave an admiring gasp. Then he cursed again and eased his foot down. The Bentley was far ahead, a diminishing blue shape. Hood settled more grimly than ever at the wheel. He imagined the girl's wet mauveish mouth smiling her amused smile and saying something that he would laugh at himself.

She had given him the smile and the come-on when they had stopped alongside each other in Bordeaux. They had both, in their respective cars, just left the town behind. She had not, of course, known that he had come a long way to pursue her. They had crossed the Garonne and were headed towards the N10 when they had been held up at the level crossing.

She had looked at Hood – a tall powerfully built man whose dark brown hair was inclined to curl. He had small fan-wise creases at the corners of his eyes when he smiled.

Hood had looked back at her. She was stamped with great chic – a natural blonde with hair done in the careless elegance of one of the great coiffeurs. Her eyebrows arched rather high and wide over her blue eyes. She had on a printed dress with a rounded neck. The mauve-tinted lipstick was perfect for her. Sitting in the car, she looked as if she might be tall. Above all, her effect was humorous and entertainingly frivolous. Who could want more?

She lit a cigarette and looked at him obliquely. Their

eyes met. They contained smiles of amused appreciation. She pouted her lips, taking out the cigarette deeply rouged. Her shoulder lifted slightly. She knew the game all right.

'Baby,' Hood said to himself. For an instant, the assignment, the grim official reason for his pursuing her, receded. He held her look. She was the sort of girl who gave glamour to places and meetings; who would stamp any moment with her own magic. She was irresistibly a 'presence', and Hood, for one, could hear her music.

The train appeared. It was some shunting operation. The gates remained shut. Hood took in the girl's car. It was a Continental Bentley but she had had a Rolls-Royce radiator fitted and the bonnet adjusted to take it, the hubcaps changed and the Bentley sign removed astern. But Hood noticed the rev counter to her right on the dashboard. It could only mean Bentley since there was none on a Rolls. It looked as if she had made the changes for a joke.

The gates lifted. The girl tossed her cigarette out. He had one last glimpse of her profile, those wet lips. Then they moved forward.

They negotiated the traffic. She was in front. The Bentley had a crackly exhaust which sounded fixed too. Then, going up the winding climb beyond the town to the highway, she started to zip it up.

To begin with, Hood had easily kept on her tail. The stretch from Bordeaux to Angoulême was a switchback of ups and downs. Besides, there were enough lorries to keep their speed under 70. Just before Angoulême he had been held up briefly by a manoeuvring trailer and lost her. But in the town itself he had caught her again.

Then she had really started to race. She took no risks; but she moved round the *rond-point* and out of Angoulême at a deceptively fast pace that had him checking and hanging up for traffic while she moved smoothly and confidently on. She extended her lead, as though she weren't trying. Damn the girl, Hood thought. And that had been the beginning of the pursuit. He thought she would stop for lunch. But she had gone relentlessly on.

Now he saw he was closing again. The Bentley was held up by traffic. A sign said Ruffec 3. He was about five hundred yards behind her. Then there was the speed limit disc and they went primly down the main street.

Two motards of a traffic patrol were standing by their machines; they didn't seem much interested in the Bentley or the DS. It was a blazing autumn day, the Indian summer stretching unbelievably into late September.

Hood dropped the window for air while he could. Blinds in the town were down everywhere. Dogs lay stretched out in the dirt. A man slept on a bench with a beret over his face.

The next minute they were through and the Bentley was crackling away down the long straight tree-lined road ahead.

Hood shut the window and gave the DS everything. But that elegant Mulliner backside ahead seemed to mock him. His speedometer registered 145 kilometres, then 150. The road was dead straight, flat and clear. She was drawing away. He squeezed up to 152 – 94 miles an hour.

The dappling of the leaves danced on the surface of the road. His eyes became hypnotized by that diminishing turquoise blob. The straightness and dullness of the road were numbing. The car was hot. At moments he seemed to be floating in a vacuum. He flashed past an occasional car drawn up on the verge. Blurred figures stared. One couple had set up a table and chairs for lunch.

The Bentley was still in sight. Hood thought he had gained on it. The girl had checked slightly at a crossroads. Hood flashed across, reading the sign: La Scie. If he could hold her on this stretch, he could hold her on any other they were going to meet. No doubt of it, he had closed on her. Hood grinned. She was giving up. It was surrender. He would go ahead at the next built-up area and at a suitable point flag her to a stop. He would suggest a drink – and take it from there.

She was about eight hundred yards ahead. He checked his speed. A lorry with its tarpaulin flapping loose was coming towards them. Just as the Bentley cleared it, Hood saw something fall. It hit the road, somersaulted and started rolling – a big metal drum. Hood braked. The drum zigzagged along the crown of the road, the lid came off and a yellowish liquid spread.

Hood waved the lorry to stop as he pressed his foot down. It was paint – thick and oily. The drum had rolled to the near side and the paint was extending in a pool.

The DS responded beautifully to the brakes, digging into the road as if a giant hand were pressing on it. It pulled up yards short of the paint slick. Looking back, Hood saw that the lorry had stopped. The driver and his mate had heads out of the cabin, craning back. They got down, stood in the road.

Hood cursed with impatience. To yell would only start some idiotic shouting match. He waited until they climbed up again, turned the lorry – taking their time – and started back to deal with the situation; then, swinging out to avoid the drum and paint, he sped the DS forward.

The car settled back for speed. But he was afraid it was goodbye to the girl. He had lost minutes. He trod steadily on the accelerator.

The blonde in the Bentley looked into the driving mirror. Still no DS. She smiled. She let the Bentley drop to sixty, then to forty. After a minute or two, she braked, checked behind, backed and turned the car down a narrow dirt road between fields.

It was a farm track. There was grass in the middle and tall grasses and white-flowering weeds on either side bordering the fields. Here and there were trees. They made patches of bright sun and shade in the dirt.

The girl nosed the car slowly down the track for about a hundred and fifty yards and stopped. She switched off the engine. The quiet of the autumn countryside crept in. She took out a packet of Marlboro cigarettes, lit one and blew out a long jet of smoke.

She leant an elbow out of the driving window and sat looking back towards the N10. Cars and lorries went by. But there wasn't much traffic at this hour. Then the grey DS surged past at high speed and went swooping on down the long straight road. The girl had the barest glimpse of Hood at the wheel. Smiling, with hand on chin, she watched the car disappear.

She smoked a little more of the cigarette. Then she stubbed it and got out of the Bentley. Even without her shoes, she was tall. She stretched luxuriously. At the top of the stretch she let out a feline sound of satisfaction, a sort of purring miaow.

She stood leaning against the car, one stockinged foot hooked back against it. She was thinking what a cosy spot it was and how good it would be to make love there. She felt like love. 'M'mm,' she said to herself. 'Right here and now.'

She was smiling. Everything was still. The sounds of insects rose about her. A lark was fluttering overhead. There was nobody in sight, only the occasional passing traffic on the road beyond.

She pushed herself away from the car, walked round it, glancing right and left. She got back into the car and moved it about twenty yards farther down the path, slewing it round. Then she got out and began unhooking her dress at the side.

She crossed arms and peeled it off and tossed it into the open door of the car. She had on a pouter-pigeon French Lou bra, small blue silk pants and seamless stockings. The sun struck warmly on her skin, she stretched again. Her shoulders were broad.

Then her hands were unfastening the stockings, back and front. She let herself tip backwards through the open door on to the seat and stripped the stockings off. She sat there for a moment, legs apart, in the sun. Slowly, she let herself recline backwards on the seat until she was lying flat, legs outside, the blue pants and her smooth belly lifted.

'M'mm,' she murmured. She straightened, stood and looked round once. She let a car go by on the road, though she could hardly be seen from it. She reached back, unhooked the bra and let it loose with a little rounding of her shoulders. Holding it from the front, she lifted it away.

Her breasts swayed a little as she threw the bra in. She looked over her shoulder and a curve caressingly brushed the doorpost. Without pausing, she bent and stripped the pants off. Underneath was a narrow strip suspender belt. She took that off too.

Her body was slim, young and appetizing. Her skin had the faintest pigmentation like the last trace of suntan. She saw a small blue flower and stooped to pick it. She took two steps to the long grass, dropped to her knees and then stretched full length on her back.

She extended her arms on either side, crooking one knee. She looked up at the sky, smiling. She had been amusing herself with the DS pursuit at first. Then she had decided she had to drop him, though she rarely missed a chance.

Lying there, she gave another feline purr. He had been a good-looker too.

A tiny insect alighted on her left breast and crawled on to the pink crest. Lazily, the girl's hand came up and caressed the curve. It brushed the insect away. The crest had responded.

Heat shimmered from the roadway. The DS topped another rise. There was one retreating Dauphine a mile off.

'Oh, the hell,' Hood said and eased his foot up. He had lost her. A road sign said twenty kilometres to Poitiers. He had spent two and a half hours going back down the road and returning on the chance of having missed her at a service station or what-all. He gave up.

He was furious. He hadn't lunched. He had been chasing vainly about the hot countryside all afternoon. He was tired and he needed a drink. The contest between the cars or their driving skill had not mattered a damn to him, he told himself; nor was it deflated pride at being beaten by a girl. But there were all the other supremely important reasons for the pursuit. It was a disaster that she had got away. It was bad enough that ICC had warned him too late; but he had simply not counted on the Bentley.

He pulled into the drive of an establishment proclaiming itself a motel. There was a long curving black marble bar and a low ceiling with conical lights. Tables, a snack counter, dining area and rubber plants.

He ordered a martini.

'Yes, sir,' said the keen crew-cut executive who was serving as barman.

'Dry,' Hood said.

'Uh?' the executive said, turning back as if Hood had solicited him.

'Avec du gin,' Hood said.

'Du gin?'

'Oh God,' Hood said under his breath, 'here we go again.'

'Un martini-gin, vous voulez dire?'

'No.'

'Mais un martini, vous m'avez dit.'

Hood told him. He might have been describing a Polynesian nut-drink. Finally the young man produced a mixture in a very shallow glass. No lemon peel or olive. Hood sipped. It was warm and the amount of gin in it wouldn't have hurt a suckling infant.

He sighed and lit a cigarette. He felt baffled and ashamed at having let the girl get away. He was too hot and sticky to drive on to Paris or the coast. He felt like a bath, a good dinner and a restorative end to the day.

He looked at his watch; ten to five. He thought with pleasure of Gaston's, his favourite inn on the Vienne not far from Chauvigny. Its expensive elegance, its remoteness, the food he could count on and the likelihood that he wouldn't meet anybody there, were exactly what he needed. He could have dinner on the brick terrace in the cool of the evening with a bottle of Gaston's Romanée-Conti. Then he would drive on to Paris and report this dismal result. Decidedly that was it.

He finished the drink and went out. The glare of the afternoon came up from the gravel. It seemed as hot as ever. There was a roar and a gigantic red trailer went by, then another. Cirque Pinder. Le Plus Grand Cirque du Monde. There was a smell of oil and exhaust.

Hood climbed into the DS, pulled over to the petrol pump and filled up. He drove back through Poitiers and turned off sharp left along the small GC3 road across the plain towards the Forest of Moulière. He took his time. Among the trees it was cool and fresh. He let the Citroën dawdle. Deep silent paths ran into the ferns and undergrowth. This had been one of François Ier's great hunting domains.

He decided to go out of his way a bit and instead of branching off at the fork in the forest road, he went on; there was a bridge at Bonneuil, the next village. It would simply mean driving back a few kilometres along the river.

In the open beyond the trees, he passed the village cemetery and earth-walled barns. The street curved. He came out at the river, circled the elm, swung the nose of the Citroën at the bridge and gently braked. There was a flicker of astonishment on his face; then he grinned. The narrow stone bridge was blocked by a Dauphine and the turquoise Bentley.

'Well I'll be damned,' Hood said, continuing to grin. He had imagined her miles on, in Tours at least, or Paris.

The blonde was standing listening to a young man, evidently the owner of the Dauphine. He was showing the male indignation which the French regard as obligatory after a mishap. She was smoking a cigarette and looked amused. One or two villagers were looking on.

Hood watched the girl. She was a good-looker all right and there was that indefinable thing about her which you could only call glamour. He pulled up the hand-brake, got out and walked over. The girl looked up. She smiled frankly.

'Oh, hello. Galahad!'

'This is how flashy drivers end up.'

She laughed. He was bigger than she'd thought. Thirty-five, she guessed. Sophisticated and probably not married. She noticed his good-looking hands.

Hood thought how cool and chic she looked. 'What happened?'

'Oh, our friend here has just got his new Dauphine and had a bash.'

The villagers were looking up puzzled at the exchange in English. The young man had a shock of hair on the top of his head and a raw but good-natured look. He was in his best suit. It appeared he was the local grocer and this was his second run out with his brand-new Dauphine after passing his test. Hood felt sorry for him, poor devil – and he thought the girl did too. The Bentley had been almost over the bridge when, coming from the other side, the grocer had decided there was room for two and he could get by. He had misjudged the space. The Dauphine had a crumpled wing and a smashed headlight. The Bentley had a shallow dent in the bumper, and scratches.

'Can I help?' Hood said.

One of the bystanders was the *garde champêtre*. He had agreed to do duty for the gendarmes who were in the next village. They freed the two cars and cleared the bridge. There was the usual protracted note-taking and examination of the damage. Hood walked over to the Bentley with the girl.

'Now that I've rescued you from a hostile population, let's have dinner together.'

She smiled. 'Since you finally caught up, why not?'

'How about going to Gaston's? Shall I lead the way?'

'Won't it look as if I'm pursuing?' She laughed.

'I hope it does.'

She got into the car. 'Lead on, then.'

Hood drove across the bridge and turned down the

road alongside the river. She followed. Twenty minutes later they were turning through the gates into the flagged courtyard of Gaston's under the trees.

Gaston's was one of the places Hood always returned to with pleasure. It was a mill-house which in Revolutionary times had been built on to a sixteenth-century priory, all since restored with great care and, here and there redesigned. It was *classé* by the Beaux Arts. Gaston, who owned it, was small and plump. He had started life as a bell-boy at the Ritz when he was fourteen and he was one of the great hoteliers of Europe. But he was only happy operating on a small scale. Gaston's was never advertised. Its supreme comforts were passed on by word of mouth to the very few.

The girl got out and looked round admiringly and did a little twirl. They went in. It was a sumptuous long room with settees in green Genoa velvet, a monumental stone fireplace with a Giacometti figure beside it, an Aubusson carpet, a Chinese lacquer screen and windows looking out on to the river. Gaston had just put in three seventeenth-century Spanish doors which looked very good.

Gaston came up. He caught a small sign from Hood. So instead of saying, 'Well, Mr Hood, this is a great pleasure,' he smiled and said: 'Good evening, Monsieur. Fortunately it is a little cooler now.'

'How are you, Gaston? We'd like to have dinner; but that's something we can discuss later.'

'Oh, I like this!' The girl went forward exclaiming admiringly. She spun on a heel. 'I'd like to stay tonight – if there's a room?'

'Of course, Mademoiselle.'

Hood glanced at her. This was a shade unexpected – and promising.

There were the preliminaries with baggage and the cars. 'I need a drink,' Hood said. He went through to the terrace while the girl chose a room and installed herself. Gaston came up bringing Hood's double martini himself. 'Your usual room, Mr Hood?'

'Yes, please, Gaston. Is that all right?'

'Perfectly.'

Hood sipped the perfect martini, finished his cigarette and carried the drink upstairs. His bath was running. He put the drink on the edge, undressed, got in and lay back. He reached out for the martini and drank.

This was, he admitted, the exact situation he had wanted to bring about. It was what he had been expected to manage. Yet for once he found he was uncertain of the outcome. The girl was a fast mover. She obviously knew she was playing dangerously. She was intelligent and would do the unexpected. He would have to play it as it came.

He dressed and went downstairs. The girl came out on to the terrace. Hood got a small shock of pleasure. She was wearing a Thai silk dress in shades of brown with one round silver Kashmir brooch set with agates – extremely chic.

'A highball,' she said.

'It's a lovely place here. Are you one of the habitués?'

'No, Mademoiselle. Mademoiselle what?'

'Joyce Antrim. I suppose I call you Mr Citroën? Dudley Stuart?' She laughed.

'As a matter of fact, my name is Charles Royce,' Hood lied. 'And I was pursuing you to find out why you've disguised that souped-up Bentley.'

'My delicious Rolls? *Un*souped up.'

Time went with great speed. They were alone at dinner on another part of the terrace and she was very attractive. There were discreet lights. The river shimmered like dark green silver and made soft sounds. They had *saumon en pâte* with which Hood chose a 1945 Pouilly-Fuissé and a *gigue de chevreuil* and *paillasson truffé* with a '43 Romanée-Conti. It was food for the gods.

She was amusing and obviously having fun. To Hood the combination was exciting. But she eluded him expertly. When he tried to find out what she had been doing, she laughed. She had been 'seeing friends', and all his testing and probing got no farther. She knew any number of people he knew in London and Paris and elsewhere – but Hood didn't want to press any of that too closely and sheered off when names came up. She was moderately inquisitive about him. But when Hood spoke of merchant banking and his life in the City, she laughed sceptically and he couldn't help grinning. She was full of laughter and very gay.

They rose and strolled out. Their hands touched. He put her hand to his lips, kissed her inside the neck of her dress. He felt her hand exploring his chest. She laughed, pushed him away. In the courtyard, the moonlight made blocks of shadow.

'Let's go and see the chateau park,' Hood said.

'All right. Whose chateau?'

'It belongs to the Villemombles. Nobody can live in the place. It has about eighty rooms and needs thirty gardeners. The Villemombles have been trying to unload it on the State for years. It has a park and a *pièce d'eau*. Gaston keeps the keys.'

They took the Bentley. 'You drive,' she said.

They ran up a sloping road. At the end, the headlights showed a pair of high ornamental iron gates. Hood got out and went over, unlocked one and swung it screeching back. There were alarmed flutterings in the trees above. The girl drove the car through, stopped and Hood shut the gates again. As he got back into the driving seat, she leaned over and switched the headlights off. 'Better,' she said. Hood looked at her. The dashboard lights were on and the moisture of her mauve lips gleamed faintly. She was looking straight ahead, as if not noticing the pause, though he knew she was. He kissed her neck and turned back to drive.

The wide tree-lined avenue was interspersed with bright patches of moonlight. There wasn't a breath of wind. Hood moved the car forward. At the end of the drive they came to a big open space, full of moonlight, and the chateau in the distance. A stone parapet ran along a branch of the river. There were side alleys and statues which made faint white figures. They got out and strolled along the alleys. She began fooling; then ran back and jumped up on the stone parapet.

'Don't be an idiot. Get down!' he said. She kicked off her shoes. He stepped in to grab her and she jumped and he caught her. She looked down at him, sliding down in his arms.

He kissed her. She wound her arms round his neck. The shock of her lips was cool. She dug her hands hard into his shoulder. When they released each other, she was breathless. She put her face against his chest; she was pressed to him.

She whispered something he couldn't hear.

'Joyce.' He lifted her chin and kissed her again. They sat on the stone bench near by. She was wonderfully exciting. The skin above her stocking stirred him. Her leg was raised from the bench, bent at the knee. He was aware, in the faint light, of the long uncovered leg. She raised it against him.

'Charles – no!' She released herself and laughed, gave in for a moment again, then struggled away. But the next minute she had her arm round his neck. 'I mean, yes – but —'

'But what?'

'Not here.'

'Why not? Come here.'

'Oh, darling, because —'

'What?'

'Because I have a special thing about love. Are you going to be sweet and make love to me?'

'Come here and see.' She was on her feet, shaking down the dress.

'You come over here.'

He got up. But she eluded his grasp and ran to the car. He followed her and she took his shoulders.

'What's this special thing about love-making?' Hood said.

She laughed. 'Darling – I've got a special sense of place! I keep on being tempted by different places. I keep seeing somewhere new and I can't help thinking oh, I'd like to make love there. Sometimes I think if I don't make love there, I won't get another chance! Once it was on an operating table. So thrilling! Infinite adjustments. Twiddle a knob here, twiddle a knob there. Then once I couldn't resist a lovely snowdrift.'

'What can't you resist now?'

She didn't answer. They kissed.

'Wait a minute.' She released herself and ran a hand caressingly over the helmet wing at the graceful stern of the car, smoothing up one side and down the other. 'Just the angle – and this top ridge.'

Hood grinned. 'Is that a special?' But she turned and got into the car. When Hood made to follow, she called out mockingly: 'Stay there. I am turning myself into Lady Godiva.'

A moment after, she came out. She was holding her dress in front of her, just below her nude shoulders. She came up smiling, holding the dress with flattened palms to her breast. She slid in between him and the wing and stood there before him looking at him. It was a perfect seduction act. Hood admitted – but done with humour and grace and her special magic. As she reached up and put both arms round his neck and the dress fell, Hood took hold of her.

Her head went back. She held him, leaning backwards over the car's gliding stern. One of her knees moved gently against his side. Hood was swept on with irresistible passion.

She broke the kiss, breathless again.

'Charles . . .' She was full of enthusiasm and made small ecstatic sounds and dug her nails into him. Hood was completely carried away. She was half fighting him and half impelling him farther, pulling him in to her with both arms, then the knee which had been pressed against him slowly relaxed, her arms loosened a little. Presently her feet were touching the ground.

One of her arms hung down loosely.

'You hurt me,' she said. 'But it was . . . m'mmm . . .'

He kissed the line of her jaw. 'At least you've eliminated that place.'

'Bentleys' are wonderful engineers.'

He laughed.

'In the meantime, you are breaking my back along this ridge.'

'It's your ridge and you've got to lie on it. I've a good mind to keep you here till the morning and the cows arrive.'

She said: 'I was sunbathing today and a cow dribbled on me.'

'Why have you been concealing things from me all evening and not telling me where you've been?'

'Darling – let sleeping girls lie.'

He laughed. She said: 'If you don't get off I shall become encrusted.'

They moved. She picked up the dress, reached into the car and stood behind the open door putting her things on. In a minute, Hood went up. She was hoisting a stocking, fixing the top to a suspender. He had another stab of desire for her and moved round the door and picked her up.

She said: 'I don't know anything about you, if it comes to that – except that we could go places together!' She laughed. 'Give me a cigarette and let's go down to that chateau.'

Hood put her down and lit her cigarette. They drove the Bentley down to the great house looming against the mass of trees. But for some reason, Hood's keys didn't fit any of the doors and they walked round looking up at the high façade with the windows shining from the moon. There was a round stone tower at one end. A night bird flew off with a shriek.

'The house is full of trophies. Georges Villemomble is a great sportsman.'

'Darling!' She stopped and stood in front of him. 'Can't we break in?'

'Break in?'

'A tiger-skin rug is one of my most coveted places.'

'Let's go back and see if Gaston's got one in the attic.'

It was midnight. The Bentley purred softly into Gaston's courtyard. There were a few shaded lights in the downstairs rooms.

She got the key of her room and went up. Hood asked Henri, the night porter, to bring a pint of Roederer and stood on the terrace looking out on the river while he fetched it. Henri retreated. Hood waited a moment, then carried the bucket upstairs.

He knocked at her door. She opened a crack, then let him in. She was wearing a slinky wrapper. He smelt Dior's Diorling and the complex smell of a woman's bedroom. Hood crossed the room, put the champagne down and looked round. She was turning the key in the lock.

Hood woke up in his own bed at 7.05 o'clock. The sun was blazing in at the open window. He had left the curtains undrawn when he had come back two hours before, so that the daylight would help wake him. But his faculty of being able to set his mind like a clock and wake at a given hour had worked perfectly.

He felt pleasantly tired, the sort of numbed and pervasive sense of well-being a man feels after a night of love-making. He could have slept till noon, but he had decided he could not afford a chance of losing the girl again now.

He got out of bed, rang room service and ordered black coffee. He could have breakfast downstairs once he was posted where he could see her come down, or at least see the Bentley. When the waiter came with the coffee, he was under the shower.

'Lovely morning, sir.'

'Looks splendid.' Hood grabbed the bathrobe and went out. He poured the coffee, took the cup and crossed with it to the window. He stood drinking and looked out on to the lawn along the river bank.

Now, he thought, came the tough part. The girl was beautiful and frivolous and full of gaiety. But for all their love-making, she had put up an excellent defence against his knowing more about her and, what he needed to know above all, where she had been and where she was going. She had turned him aside deftly and cleverly whenever he had approached these things and made it seem ponderous that he should pursue it. It obviously wasn't going to be easy to stay with her. He would have to search her baggage and so forth.

He finished the coffee and dressed without wasting time. He went downstairs and out into the courtyard. They had taken the Bentley to the garage. Gaston was coming from the garden. He had a rose in his hand. 'Is everything in order, Mr Hood? You are comfortable?'

'Absolutely, Gaston.'

'They say we are in for bad weather. It doesn't look it.'

Hood said: 'Do you know if Mademoiselle Antrim has come down yet?'

'She has left, Mr Hood. She went very early this morning. About five o'clock.'

Hood drove to Paris with the sky turning grey and threatening. It was beginning to rain when he reached the office of the French subsidiary of the ICC. He was shown to the private suite and put in a call to Lord Claymore in London.

'Fifteen minutes' wait, sir,' the telephone girl said.

'Very well.' He hung up.

There was a flurry of rain against the window. Decidedly it looked like the end of the Indian summer. Outside, the traffic was coagulating in the Place de la Concorde. Immense flags in green and red – some African state – stirred heavily at the great metal masts the Gaullists had put up on the Tuileries side and on the rows more opposite. Hood thought they were hideous. The jammed cars and the sense of chaos this city so often gave intensified his grim feelings.

When the telephone rang, there was a brief pause, then Claymore came on.

'Well? What does she say?'

'I'm sorry, we were out of luck. She got away.'

'Oh, my God.'

'We were told too late. When I arrived at the hotel she was already pulling out and I had to chase her.'

'Where'd she been before that?'

'Don't know.'

'Or where she went afterwards?'

'I couldn't discover. She is charming – and clever as hell. I've been casting about in the area; but there is nothing doing.'

'You've got to find her, Charles!'

'I confess I think she is fooling with somebody. But how far it has gone beyond indiscretion, I don't know.'

'But who – *who*?'

'I hate to tell you who I think it is.'

'What do you mean?' Claymore's voice was harsh. 'Who is it?'

Hood stabbed his cigarette in the glass ashtray. He knew Claymore wasn't going to like this. 'Zagora.'

'Good God.' Claymore's voice was a whisper. 'How do you know?'

'Oh – things she said, a hint here and there, an allusion. It's only suspicion and I may be wrong. I snooped round his house near Fontainebleau but it is shut up.'

'That man!' Claymore spoke very softly. 'He has done untold harm. He is a teacher of corrupt and dangerous things. He has led an enormous number of good women astray; and I needn't tell you that they include the most distinguished and talented women in society. It's sickening, it's hideous to contemplate the position he has achieved. I hear of him insidiously and constantly – and they always talk about him as if he were a saint.'

'They're supposed to be close to the devil.'

The line hummed faintly. Claymore said: 'I have had to tell the PM, Charles. A few minutes before you came through he was on to me. He was in a bloody jagged mood and it was not pleasant. In the end, I got some of the edge off – though on the strength of what, God knows. For the moment he only knows the outline and he finally said he is confident if you are handling it. You've got to find her, Charles; call in your security friends, whoever you like.'

'Very well.'

'Good luck – for all our sakes.' Claymore rang off.

Hood got up. He lit a fresh cigarette and paced the office. He looked out again on the tangled traffic below – damnably symbolic. Then he turned and put in another call to London, this time to Conder at Special Intelligence Security, the innermost Government secret agency for which he worked.

When it came through, Conder said: 'I've been trying to reach you. Are you on a scrambler?'

'No. I'm speaking from ICC.'

'There's been an attempt to kidnap the other girl here. Bogus call to a hospital. Cleverly done. Fortunately we were in time. What luck with you?'

'She got away. I've told Claymore.'

'Hold on.' Conder put the phone down. There were noises off and a prolonged wait. Hood could hear voices. At last Conder came back. 'I've just been given a signal. Private Beechcraft Super H 18 left Bordeaux Merignac with three men and girl on stretcher this afternoon. They covered up very fast, but from what we make out they headed for Venice.'

'Venice? Then it's Zagora?'

Conder's voice was grim. 'I hate to say so, Charles, but it looks like it.'

CHAPTER FOUR

THE AIR FRANCE CARAVELLE was flying rock-steady at 25,000 feet. The weather at this altitude was brilliantly clear.

'Something to drink, sir?' the hostess said to Hood.

'A whisky and soda,' Hood said, and added hastily, 'no ice.'

She turned into the forward area to mix it, dutifully twitching the curtain behind her. Hood abandoned *Le Monde* and lit a cigarette.

'Mesdames, Messieurs, on the left you can see the city of Geneva,' the voice said in French over the announcement system, then repeated it in the incomprehensible airline English.

He glanced out at the lake and the runways in the brown and grey rug of country below. Thousands of feet beneath them a tiny silver plane was turning in mid-air, like a small silver fish swimming very fast.

The hostess brought the drink. 'Thanks,' Hood said. She smiled, ready for a chat. This was the off-season for the Venice run; there was only one other passenger in the first class and she hadn't much to do.

Hood sipped the drink and settled into his seat. He had about an hour, a small interregnum between now and whatever lay ahead. He wished he felt happier about the job. But the thing had started badly and now he couldn't shake off the feeling that the assignment was stamped with disaster.

His mind went back two weeks to the briefing from Conder. Hood had spent the morning going over the file on Zagora, they had lunched at Brooks's and gone back to the SIS office afterwards.

'Well, you've seen the dope,' Conder said. 'I don't know that I can tell you much more. Zagora's a many-sided man. That stuff about his being known as The Monk Zagora or Father Zagora is the sort of thing that must infuriate the orthodox atheists among his masters – I mean the idea, at this late date, that the Revolution should be using methods that remind you of the holy men of Dostoevsky's novels or Rasputin. You can imagine them sitting in the great grey office blocks of their arch-bureaucracy feeling damned uncomfortable about him. He must seem like a whiff of the superstitious past they haven't yet managed to root out.

'He was probably born in the frontier region beyond Lake Baikal; but we don't know where. He's obviously a peasant by origin and seems to have spent an early period of his life as a wanderer. At the end of it he appeared as a "holy man". He did penances and fasted, attracted attention and of course was arrested.

'This was where Zagora's real career began. As the story goes, he made a profound impression on the security police at the interrogations. Besides his personality and his natural shrewdness, the years of wandering had given him uncanny insight into human nature. He had cultivated himself and developed great powers of mental penetration.

'You've read what the file says about the police passing him on to the Party and so on. The Fourth Bureau took him up, gave him special training and inserted him into the priesthood. We think this is the same man who was placed as a sleeper in the Rumanian town of Sibiu for a time.

'At this period, Zagora – if it were he – lived the life of a humble orthodox priest. He wore the black robes. His great silver cross hung on his chest and he had his long hair parted in the middle in the fashion of Christ. He had hardly a penny. He wandered again on pilgrimages to holy places and ministered to those poorer even than himself. Devout followers had gathered to him. It was said that he effected cures and did remarkable things. Women came to him in trouble or to listen to him.

'During the war he disappeared. Afterwards, as you've seen, he turned up in Austria. He had given up the priesthood and established himself as a guru, a mystic.'

'His masters were enlarging his role?'

Conder shrugged. 'At all events, reports of his earlier holy life and his mysterious powers soon spread. People came to him as before; but this time they were the rich, not the poor – and above all, they were women.'

Conder paused. He was curiously engagé, Hood always thought, for a professional spy-killer. Conder hated the other side; and there was a purity about his attitude.

He wasn't hard-bitten or grey or bleak about the grim and seedy world he lived in, as so many of them were.

Conder went on: 'Since his earliest days as a holy man, Zagora has had an enormous hold over women – not merely women past their prime or frustrated dowagers. There were also chic and beautiful young women of the best society who came to the master's feet from Paris, Rome, Stockholm, London, New York, Lisbon – all over. He became a fashionable guru. You could, as you have, Charles, hear him talked of in the Avenue Foch, in Eaton Square, in the East Sixties, in Strandvägen, in the Via Giulia.

'Everything, of course, has been done with great skill and discretion. Zagora has put up all sorts of barriers against newcomers. It's been extremely difficult from the first to join the circle of his disciples. Zagora knew this was the way to still higher spheres and he intended exercising a close selection. Vanity, of course, impels the women to let it be known that they are among the chosen. But jealousy keeps them from wanting to share their guru with social rivals and so they don't say too much. The protective system has become self-organizing. Husbands who might frown find their inquiries evaded and aren't usually curious enough to try to penetrate this "woman's world". But other men have obviously been led to Zagora by wives or daughters and come under his direct influence; and probably still more are worked on without their knowing it.'

Hood said: 'The file said something about the methods of the *klysti*. What's that?'

'The *klysti* were an anti-orthodox Siberian sect who had a great clandestine following at one time. Their monks and martyrs preached the attainment of sanctification through sin.'

'That explains plenty!'

'It's a pretty ancient doctrine. It must have revolted the Party boys at home, but Zagora has got away with it.'

Hood said: 'What does he do?'

Conder stubbed out his cigarette. 'We think – we

think – he's a special sort of offensive agent. He has probably developed a lot of the technique himself. I don't see him simply gathering data like any damned cultural attaché or UN chauffeur, though I dare say he accepts what comes his way. We have a feeling he is doing something much more subtle, more complex – something much more difficult to counter.'

'Such as?'

Conder paused. He seemed to be searching for a way to formulate a complicated process. 'Leaking damaging facts ... planting misleading information ... harmful rumours – not just about political affairs but about international business, industrial processes, the activities, interests and intentions of European firms.'

'Would it do 'em any good?'

'Sure. There have been any number of awful cock-ups lately – blunders, new feuds, if you look back over things.'

Hood watched him.

'A whole complex of things has been leading us to this conclusion. The file doesn't cover it because it's too diffuse and too widespread and we've only just begun to put two and two together. But the signs point to Zagora being immensely skilful in compromising people.

'We are gradually getting an image of Zagora as a man who has become a past master in discrediting, say, a Cabinet Minister in one country, attaching suspicion to a senior adviser in another, destroying confidence in a key man elsewhere, prematurely disclosing a financial operation or disrupting associations which are potentially harmful to his masters. If Zagora knows from the inside exactly the steps to take to sow misunderstanding, confusion and rivalry, he can do immense harm. Christ! It's hard enough to get along as it is with the ordinary jostling and power-seeking in politics and industry without somebody actively stirring it up. Mind you, he probably also controls agents who settle matters by more direct methods.'

'What's this hide-out of his in the Dolomites?' Hood said.

'Don't know. Not even sure where it is. Supposed to be somewhere north of Venice.'

'The file mentions Diana Undermere, but I couldn't see — '

'No. The papers have been out.' Conder lit a new cigarette. 'There was a sadistic incident at the house near Fontainebleau which these women have given him. Zagora was charged with rape. Somehow or other he or his friends got it squashed and the affair dissolved into nothing, as these things can in France. Much later we heard that the girl had been Diana Undermere, but in the meantime she had died. She had been seeing Zagora – "my teacher" as she called him – for some time beforehand.'

'Anything in her death?' Hood said.

'She was alone – died at a hotel, as a matter of fact. Natural causes. Certified as heart failure and extreme exhaustion. One of the doctors, we found out, had mentioned something called laughing death.'

'Good God.'

'It's a mysterious disease of the central nervous system. Pretty bloody awful. You just go on uncontrollably laughing till you die. Nobody knows much about it. Anyway, nobody wanted to follow it up. And she *had* died of heart failure, so the certificate was accurate enough in a sense. You can imagine them all wanting to soft-pedal it like mad, to avoid complications. Her parents were in Bolivia, somewhere inaccessible. By the time we came in it was all done with. Her aunt had gone over, had the body cremated and flown back with the ashes. It was all entirely legal and everybody had behaved impeccably – only we got the impression that the formalities had been settled good and quick.'

'Anything else?'

Conder threw him a look. 'Only one more thing. It's not an official record – but Zagora's a killer.'

Now, with the hostess taking his empty whisky glass,

Hood remembered the coldness of Conder's voice. The outlook was unpleasant.

The aircraft was beginning its descent. There was the shudder as the air brakes came on. They dropped smoothly for the approach with the sun flashing on the green and yellow patchwork of waterlogged fields. The Dolomites beyond, like the cones of an enormous Neanderthal anti-tank block, lifted out of sight over the wing. Venice itself was invisible.

The metallic voice of the hostess was coming over the announcement system. '...Kindly keep your seats and refrain from smoking until...'

There was the bump and bounce of the touch-down and the aircraft taxied to a stop. On the tarmac the sun shone strong and warm.

Hood walked across to the small wooden airport building feeling grateful that it wasn't one of the vast international junctions with the chimes and miles of corridors and the lost-looking airport crowds. Marco Polo airport, Venice, didn't amount to much more than a couple of largish huts. This had the extra advantage that if Graff, The Circle man, was there to meet him, he would have spotted any obvious watchers.

The tall blue-jawed Italian at Immigration stamped his passport and handed it back without question. Hood grabbed his suitcase from the bench and turned to the single young customs man opposite.

'Niente.' The young man flicked Hood a mute sad glance and chalked. Hood went through the glass door. In the outer area there were about half a dozen people and a chauffeur or two waiting near the money-changer's desk.

Hood spotted Graff's plummy, heavy-lidded face at once but looked through him. But the next minute Graff was coming towards him, smiling and extending a hand. Evidently the coast was clear.

'How are you, Arthur?' Hood shook hands with relief. He saw how much he was relying on Arthur Graff's support and expertise as the local man.

'How are you, sir?' Graff said. He was small, fat and olive-skinned with blue eyes, thin black hair, a man of infinite good temper, resource and more personal friends than any other man Hood knew. He was one of The Circle's best agents in Europe.

'Fine, Arthur. You're looking great.'

They walked out into the sun to the car. Hood said: 'By God, this is good after London. You don't know how lucky you are, Arthur.'

'Oh yes, I do, sir,' Graff said, and laughed. The car parked close by, was a big 1952 Dodge. 'I'm sorry about this, sir,' Graff said. 'I hired it from Kurtz. I thought it might be better: not so noticeable.'

'Sure, why not?'

But as Hood threw in his bag, he gave Graff a look. The old car seemed an unusual precaution, unless there was something cooking. Graff had been partly briefed but not told all the facts. Hood's uneasiness sharpened.

They turned out of the airport and drove down the flat dusty country road towards Mestre. The trees traced their delicate shadows in the dirt. They passed red-tiled farm buildings, untidy fields of maize. Then as they swung left round the roundabout and headed down the long arrow-straight causeway towards Venice, Graff gunned the big car. For all its hard use, it was well tuned. They surged forward. Hood knew he could do nothing better at this stage than leave things to Graff. Graff went on talking about a trip he had made that summer with his young wife to Gothenburg and Hood listened, giving rather automatic responses.

The sea spread on either side like dull steel. Green domes and bell-towers came in sight, then cranes and shipping on the right as they approached the end of the causeway. Then they were pulling away on to the parking area on the Piazzale Roma in front of some shops.

'That was a precaution, sir,' Graff said as he pulled out Hood's bag. 'I don't think we were tailed.'

Hood lifted his eyes over the car roof. The scene beyond, the passing cars, buses, the coach station, pedestrians told him nothing unusual. Graff gave Hood's bag to an assistant who had appeared and told him to take it on ahead.

'Let's get the *vaporetto,*' Graff said. 'I have motor-boats, of course, at your disposal. But the bus would be unobtrusive.'

'All right.'

They crossed the Piazzale Roma to the landing stage. Graff bought tickets for San Tomà, the third stop on the No 2 route, and they stood waiting for the boat. It was an exciting scene to Hood and always an exciting moment, renewal with Venice.

Beyond the turn of the canal, just hidden, awaited the gorgeous, maddening, catty city, a folding postcard, gentle, moody and unique. In anticipation, he thought of the pink palaces reflected in green side-canals, the peeling plaster, the melons, the oleanders on ancient brick. In front of them now, on this fringe, shiny brown motor-boats were nosing back and forth in the choppy water of the canal. A dust-bin barge with its curious superstructure chugged by. The noise, the movement of the boats, the slapping of the water gave the scene extraordinary animation and life. In spite of his vague worry, Hood felt the old and special lift return.

The little covered pontoon-landing stage was crowded with waiting passengers – local workmen, a couple of priests, tourists, Italian women with bundles. Graff said something and Hood bent his head to hear.

'It is curious,' Graff said. 'The hotel porter over there. The hotel changed hands recently; they have a new uniform, not that one.'

Hood took his time, then glanced round. The hotel porter in a brown uniform was standing in the corner of the landing stage. He was taking no notice of them, waiting like everybody else.

'Perhaps he's just having fun,' Hood said. But he saw that it had been a mistake to use the bus where they could be followed so easily.

They jolted gently as the black and white *vaporetto*

bumped alongside. Passengers streamed off. The porter, who was carrying a parcel, hung back and boarded the bus behind them. With grinding, vibration and shuddering, the bus chugged off. Nobody made much attempt to talk above the din. Hood was content to look out at the great brooding palaces, like ruined and ancient nobles crowded at the water's edge, and his oppression drifted away.

They ran up the Grand Canal past the Ca'D'Oro, under the Rialto bridge, past Goldini's Theatre. As the bus pulled in towards Stop 10, Graff rose. They struggled off. Just ahead of them, the porter got off too. A few yards along the quayside, he stopped to refasten the string of the parcel, balancing it on his knee. As they turned along the small quiet street to the hotel, he had gone.

'One of our friends?' Hood said.

Graff shrugged. 'It is difficult to tell.'

The hotel was separated from the street by a big paved courtyard, with statues and elegant pilasters, which ran down to a portico and terrace on the canal. It was the old Palazzo Vincenzi, at which Hood stayed when he could face the outrageous cost and wanted to be very private. It was superbly comfortable and reserved to only a few.

Giulio, the manager and part-owner, came out to greet Hood personally. He had been at Cambridge with Hood for a year. But beside their old acquaintanceship, a reservation by Rothsteil Brothers (The Circle bank, though, of course, Giulio knew nothing of The Circle) commanded special consideration. Hood was given a room on the sunny front of the house from which he could see the Grand Canal and the edge of the Palazzo Contarini.

When the servant had brought up his bag and gone, Hood lit a cigarette. 'Now, Arthur.'

'Well, sir, there's no trace of her. The plane has gone but the airport people don't remember anything about a sick woman. They're pretty easy-going, sir – you may have noticed. Private traffic gets through without much of a check. These people are good, hard-working people, but when the season's over – well, they have the winter to face.' His heavy-lidded eyes looked up at Hood for understanding, and he shrugged. Sure, thought Hood; a little bribery here, as anywhere else.

He turned to the window, came back. 'Where is Zagora's place?'

'Zagora? Joseph Zagora?'

'Yes.'

Hood noticed the abrupt change in Graff's manner. Graff had, in that moment, undergone a shock, and made a mighty effort to recover. He looked uneasily subdued. Quietly he said: 'Is he tied up with this, sir?'

'Yes. What of it?'

Graff coughed nervously, making a play with a packet of cigarettes. Hood had never seen him so scared. 'What do you know about him?' Hood said.

'What everybody knows. That he is powerful and very dangerous, that it is best to keep a distance, not to be in trouble with him.'

'What about this place of his in the mountains?'

Graff said: 'I do not know, Mr Hood. I confess I have never tried to find out. It is a lapse on my part, but sometimes it is best not to be too curious. It is somewhere on the Piave, I believe, a big place. I have no details. It is not an area where one would go prying for amusement.'

'Whereabouts on the Piave?'

'That I do not know either for certain. I have heard near Belluno.'

'It's the place where these women go? Where he teaches as a guru?'

'Yes.' Graff's brow was wrinkled unhappily. 'You will hear very little about it in Venice. Oh, the people here are no more virtuous than anywhere else. But they wish to avoid unpleasant consequences. There have been accidents to those who were indiscreet, some of them fatal. It has been impossible to trace the origin. But now people prefer to keep their mouths shut, Mr Hood.'

'I'm going up there, at all events, Arthur, wherever it is. I want you to find out all you can – and very fast.'

'I will try to find out something, Mr Hood. You will have to move very carefully.'

'Can you get a line on him quickly, Arthur?'

'I have one good friend who might be willing to help us.'

'Then will you get in touch with him straight away?'

'Yes. It is a woman.'

'How soon can you see her?'

Graff considered. 'Perhaps tonight. We will meet in Harry's Bar at 7.15. Then we will go to the Ostrich. It is a new place, a night-spot, quite notorious. It is not somewhere I should recommend, but we may find out something about Zagora there.'

He managed a smile as he left; and once again Hood noted how therapeutic had been the prospect of action on a man's fears.

Hood unpacked, got into the bath and soaked for fifteen minutes. Drying himself, he rang for the waiter and ordered a double martini. It came cold with the glass blurred by the chill and the twist of lemon-rind in it and he stood in the bathrobe drinking it and looking out on to the small side canal beneath his window and the Grand Canal beyond.

The sun was setting, the last rays gilding the domes and roofs opposite. A gondola came by, the gondolier giving the sharp awkward-looking shoves with his oar. Beyond, from the lagoon, a liner sounded its siren on an uneasy note, moaning up the buoyed channel.

But for once the drink didn't relax him. He felt keyed up. He felt that they needed to work fast, that he had no business standing there with a martini in his hand looking out on to the Grand Canal. He thought of Tiara's amused smile turning to fear.

He finished the drink and began to dress.

They had two Spanish Screwdrivers at Harry's, dined on big crisp Venetian shrimps and soft-shelled crabs and reached the Ostrich at 11.30. There was a satanic-looking bar in red silk off the street and the main room behind was done out as a rock cavern. The place was elegant and slightly vicious with an erotic floor-show. But it produced nobody Graff was looking for. They drank a pint of Heidseck Dry Monopole Brut and Hood left Graff to lie in wait.

The warm night air greeted Hood refreshingly. Above the narrow flagged street he could see the stars and at the end there was a lantern and a bridge and blocks of shadows on the walls. Everything in him lifted to this ancient and magnificent city which he loved.

He came to another bridge and leant over. One thing the abstract boys had done after all was to make people aware of the texture of things – of a stone wall, of a small area with the rusted iron making its design with the water and space. A tiny light was burning on an ex voto on the wall – artificial flowers, painted curtains, a bit of tinfoil, love. He felt the edge of loneliness and it gave a moment of melancholy. But moods were a dangerous indulgence. He snapped out of it, turned and walked back to the hotel.

Next morning he woke at six. He could not expect Graff for two hours. He shaved, dressed and went downstairs and walked through to the Piazza.

It was fresh and deserted in the morning air. A photographer with an old-fashioned tripod camera and red-lined cape was operating outside the Basilica. Hood walked through to the Riva dei Schiavoni. The *vaporetto* for the Guidecca – the island opposite – was about to leave. On impulse he jumped aboard. He stood looking back at the retreating waterfront, the great pink palace, the rocking mass of gondolas, the tugs.

The boat bumped alongside. Hood got off and turned along the quay. San Redentore church loomed ahead. The door was open. He went up the steps and entered. The church was empty. He passed down the coldly austere nave and noticed they had a new statue of the Virgin with a long rosary in light-bulbs, not attractive.

He stepped into the end chapel and was surprised to see the sacristy open too at this hour; then he remembered the effigies and went in. It was a small square room with dark wood panelling – and there, on the shelves, they were, the two rows of painted wax heads of the saints under their glass domes. The eyes turned heavenwards, the beards bristled. When the light was a little uncertain or shifting, they looked so lifelike! He had heard of tourists taking them for real bottled heads. He said good morning to Saint Seraphinus and Saint Laurentius and gave a nod to Saint Felix A Cantalico. He stood looking for a moment at the Veronese on the wall behind, then went out. On the quay he was suddenly hungry and caught the next boat back.

Graff rang him while he was breakfasting in front of the open window of his room and said he would be round in half an hour. 'I have everything.' He arrived twenty minutes late, his cheerfulness looking a bit forced, Hood thought.

'Zagora's place is called Kuan-t'eng, which is apparently an ancient word meaning The Portal.'

'A sort of Shangri-do, so to speak?' Hood said with a grin; but Graff didn't get it. 'Never mind.'

'It is up beyond Mas. That is in the province of Belluno. I have brought a map to show you.' He rather fumblingly and overhastily unfolded a map, spread it out half over the breakfast things and pointed the way. From Venice, his finger ran almost due north to Treviso, up the valley of the Piave, then northwest towards Agordo.

'Here you will find the road which passes above Mas divides about five kilometres after you have left the town. You take the upper fork and the place is along here, quite isolated. The road is not marked. You must say you have come from the Committee of Nine. If you give the name of the Baroness Van der Goot that will ensure your entry.'

'What's the Committee of Nine, for God's sake?'

'I am told they are very influential members of

Zagora's followers. They are a group which is momentarily in his favour.'

'The Baroness – anything to do with the Dutch Cabinet Minister?'

'His sister. But the words "Committee of Nine" and the Baroness's name are a recognition signal. The signal is completed by a question which you will be asked; "Are you anxious to receive teaching?" To which you must answer "Yes – to know the enlightenment of the Way." '

'I see.' Hood lit a cigarette, repeating the phrases in his mind. It was almost standard procedure so far. 'That's very good, Arthur.' He was impressed. Graff must have got close in to obtain this much. Graff, he thought, looked miserable. He looked at the map. It looked an ideal spot – an international crossroads on the frontiers of three countries, Italy, Austria and Yugoslavia, with the Adriatic near at hand. Finally he said: 'Very well, Arthur. I may need you later; if so, I'll be in touch.' He gave Graff a close look. 'What's the matter?'

'Frankly, I did not expect to get this information. I do not like it. I think it has been given to me with a purpose.'

'Yes?'

'They want to trap you.'

'That's a chance I have to take, Arthur.'

'When are you going up there?'

'As soon as you get me a good car.'

'We will go to the garage then.'

Downstairs, Hood left his personal papers with Giulio for safe keeping and they took a boat to the Piazzale Roma. Hood picked a black Mercedes 220 SE from the three cars the garage offered. The garage mechanic was anxious to make an adjustment to the lighting which he said had been giving trouble and this caused some delay. Then Hood settled in behind the wheel, said goodbye to Graff and drove off.

It was a sunny windless day. Going across the causeway, Hood tested the car's speed and found it produced 80 mph in 30 seconds; not bad. He checked his watch; it was twenty past eleven. He ought to be up above Belluno by one-thirty or two and at Mas soon after. Then it would mean locating Kuan-t'eng.

At the end of the causeway, he took the right fork up the bridge over the canal for Trieste, then after a mile turned left for Treviso. There was not much traffic. The road, lined by plane trees with thick trunks, and hoardings, ran straight between the fields of maize and vegetables. It was dusty country with greeny-greys and ochres predominating and red-tiled farm houses. The posters said: COCA-COLA IL MIGLIOR RISTORO and SUPER-CORTEMAGGIORI, LA POTENTE BENZINA ITALIANA.

He ran into Treviso, crossed the bridge over the Sile. Pulled up at the traffic lights, he watched the line of traffic coming in from the airport. He felt tense. There was a slight tingle under the surface of his mind and body which meant anticipation and danger. It was a mood he did not dislike.

He drove on. Just before he reached Vittorio Veneto, he noticed that the low grey Maserati which he had first spotted at the end of the causeway was still behind him. It was a faster car than his. Hood pulled up in the square. The Maserati went past; there were two men inside.

He got out, lit a cigarette and strolled over to the newspaper kiosk. He bought a *Stampa* and *Oggi* and stood looking at the pictures and smoking. The Maserati didn't come back. The sun shone on the dust of the square. The pictures in the papers which always conveyed to Hood the rough side of Italian life, gave their peculiar flavour. He threw the cigarette away, got into the car and drove off. He took a turning on the right and stopped at a café terrace and had a sandwich and a beer. No sign of the Maserati. He took his time and left.

Soon, beyond the town, the road began to wind up, with a steep drop on the left to the small lakes extending like pendants below the Lake of Santa Croce above. There were plenty of pines now on the slopes. This high ground was well covered, unlike the naked rock peaks of the area which lay ahead. It was like going up the Brenner, Hood thought. Then at Ponte nelli Alpi the great loop of the Piave swung in under the bridge from the left and he turned, heading along the valley.

He looked down. The Piave had once been a great river – and now it looked like the sad grey ghost of one. The hydro-electric projects had dammed up its small tributaries on either hand and the broad bed was a litter of grey stones with several small channels in the middle.

He went through Belluno. Then, as he saw the signal ahead where he would turn off for Mas, he felt a puncture on the rear near-side. His jack turned out to be a worn old Renault model which didn't work properly and he had trouble making the change. When he had done it, he ran back into Belluno, bought a new jack and filled with petrol. The episode had delayed him.

The road up past Mas was secondary and not fast. It was lateish afternoon when he went through the small town, reached the fork and swung up hairpin bends on the road above. For a stretch the road levelled. To the right there was a drop with a steep slope of rocks and sparse grass to the lower road below. On the left was a high wire link-fence lined inside with stiff matting which blocked any view. This looked like it.

Hood dropped the car to twenty. He could see nothing over the fence except the tops of occasional trees. The place was isolated up here. Then, after a bend, there was a great stone arch with high wooden doors, obviously the entrance. No sign or name. The arch looked Roman and seemed to have been transported here and re-erected. It was a fine thing – the mark of the grand seigneur to have it erected on one's own property.

Hood pulled up outside, lowered the driving window and sounded his horn. He wanted it to sound aggressive. A door in the wooden gate opened and a man stood looking at him.

'Buon giorno.' Hood said. 'Father Zagora is expecting me. Open up.' He did not smile.

The man had to bend his neck to look out of the door.

He was a heavyweight with thick dark eyebrows and no lips; not an Italian, Hood thought – and no daisy. He shut the door.

Hood sat with the engine idling. Nothing happened. He gave another blast on the horn. Still nothing. He was about to get out when the man reappeared, drew bars and bolts and swung first one side of the great doors open, then the other.

Hood swung the car and trod down – deciding to make a smash entry and rip through. But under the arch he braked hard, short of a barrier fixed across the far side. Behind him, the man slammed the doors with a boom and began making inarticulate sounds. Hood realized that he was dumb. A gatekeeper's lodge had been built under the arch. As Hood waited for the barrier to be raised, he caught sight of a tall woman behind the curtains of a window. She was holding a telephone – probably calling the house. The man went past the car into the lodge and a moment later, the barrier shot up. Hood drove in.

On the far side of the gate, the road turned sharply between low white fences. Suddenly Hood felt enormously vulnerable. Something about the reception gave him a chill in the back. It was so strong that he whipped his head round; but there was nobody visible. Nevertheless, he was in – and he felt it wasn't going to be easy to get out again.

CHAPTER FIVE

HE DROPPED the car to walking pace. A rock cliff rose on the left. The sense of remoteness was very strong. There was not a sound through the open window. Where the fences ended, the road curved to the left, round the rock, then the view opened up before him.

It was a vast, handsome place. On the left was the rock

outcrop he had just skirted; in the middle, the road ran away to a rising green mound with a big white opulent-looking house on the top of it and, to the right, above the house, a soaring jagged brown and ochre rock peak, like a claw. In the distance beyond was the circle of farther mountains.

The land was green and parklike and well kept. He passed lawns and shrubs and antique statues here and there. Grass-sprayers were turning, but there was nobody to be seen. On one wing of the house he could see a dome. The surfaced road he was on ran into a clump of ornamental shrubs and came out near the house at a different angle – and Hood braked. 'Christ!' he said under his breath.

The figure of a man on the broad terrace behind the house was beating away a big bird which was flapping close round his head. It was Zagora. Hood recognized him from the SIS pictures.

Zagora was about six feet five and naked except for a thong round his loins. The brownish tinge of his skin contrasted with his white teeth. His hair was tied in a little bun on the top of his head, like a Hindu's.

The bird was a vulture. Blusteringly it flapped off and alighted on the stone balustrade of the terrace. Zagora was laughing. He said something to the bird. His arm rose to wipe the sweat off his face; but he was not quick enough. The vulture, which had seemed so awkward and lumbering a moment before, suddenly lifted itself in a sweep of its wings and was on him. Its bald head reached forward and the beak struck out. Zagora was holding a hunk of meat in his hand. He threw himself back just in time to avoid the beak. His bellow of laughter came over. The bird was beating its wings over his head, trying to reach the meat which he kept snatching away. There seemed to be a curious interchange between them – as if both the man and the bird knew they dare not go too far, dare not provoke the other too much.

Zagora's body shone with sweat. He was twisting right and left, keeping the meat out of the bird's reach. He ducked away again from the vulture's beak and with a flick of his wrist threw the meat into one of the big ornamental stone pots on the terrace. The vulture flapped over and alighted on the edge of the pot. Its head dipped in; the neck jerked once or twice, then withdrew. It could not reach the meat, which had fallen into the pot's narrow base.

Zagora was looking on, panting and grinning. The vulture hopped down from the edge of the pot and faced him. It opened its beak and made an ugly coughing noise. Its posture became menacing. The evil eyes looked unblinkingly at the man. Zagora stopped laughing and took a step back. The bald pink head and neck sank – and Hood, looking on, thought it was going to attack.

Zagora stepped up to the great stone pot. On its pedestal, it stood a foot higher than his head. He put his shoulder to it and got his arms round it. With a mighty heave, he lifted the pot just clear of its pedestal. His neck bulged with the effort. His eyes enlarged as he strained. His white teeth were clenched in a grin.

Slowly, he tipped the pot until he was cradling it. He slid first one hand underneath, then the next. Then with his arms quivering, his legs bending at the knees with the strain, he slowly raised thc pot until he was holding it at arm's length over his head. Hood held his breath. Zagora must be tremendously strong to do that.

Then Zagora made a forward movement and hurled the pot outward. It fell with a heavy thud on the lawn beyond and broke in two. Zagora let out a short-breathed roar. The vulture flapped over to the pot, snatched the meat and flew off with it. It alighted on a tree-top fifty yards away. Zagora turned and walked back across the terrace panting and laughing and disappeared through some open french windows. Hood sat silently at the wheel for a moment. Then he engaged the gear and eased the car on. It was a shattering introduction.

The drive curved up to the house in front of a small ornamental pool. Hood got out. The bell-handle was a claw. He pulled it and waited a moment before the door was opened by a small withered man with a parchment-like face. He was barefoot and wore a belted saffron-coloured kimono. He bowed in silence, holding the door wide. Hood went into a hall with two massive columns descending in the middle from the vaulted ceiling and broad arched doorways leading off through which he caught glimpses of other columns and arches. There was an atmosphere of great luxury. The faint scent of aromatic wood burning somewhere drifted in the air. Everything was quiet.

Hood stood looking round. There was a magnificent Riccio nymph in bronze worth a fortune.

'Please, sir.' He swung round. Three pretty girls in simple high-waisted dresses and low necks, rather like the old French Directoire mode, he thought, were standing a few paces away. They were barefoot and, from the light behind them, they had nothing on underneath.

'Good evening.' On the spur of the moment, Hood didn't know how to meet this.

'You are here to see the Master?' one of the girls said.

'Yes.'

'Will you come with us?' She motioned with her hand and led the way across the hall under an arch to the next room. There was a broad low divan covered with cushions, a great candelabra with eight candles and in the middle, with a leopard-skin rug beside it, a small hexagonal pool. A fountain jet was playing in it. The decor was unusual and exotic.

'Please,' the girl said. She touched him lightly on the arm. The other two stepped forward and the next moment they were reaching up to unbutton his shirt, undo his tie, ease off his jacket.

'Hold on!' Hood said, backing but amused. 'This is extremely gracious of you, I'm sure, but – why?'

'You must be prepared, before you see the Master,' the same girl said. 'It is the rule. We are here to help you.' She had fair hair and clear blue eyes. Hood had a certain difficulty in not looking at her bosom, almost entirely revealed by the dress.

'I'm prepared, spiritually,' he said. This was a fast first move which he had not foreseen. His main concern was for his gun in the pocket at his belt.

The girl shook her head. 'It is the rule. Everyone must do so.'

Hood thought fast. It was obviously going to be a bad start to refuse. With a quick movement inside his coat, he transferred the gun from belt to breast pocket. Then he submitted with a grin.

The girls were delicate and expert and Hood felt like Abdul the Damned in his harem. They took off his shoes and socks, his shirt, lightly undid buttons and slipped his trousers off, then – with the merest aesthetic pause – in unison threw a towel over his shoulders, bustling him gently and Hood saw his elastic-sided Hongkong underpants in the fair girl's hands. It was brilliantly deft. It would have left any night-club pickpocket turn standing. Hood felt like applauding. The girl was looking at him frankly and solemnly.

'Now, please —' she said.

Hood's worry was his gun. One of the other girls was folding his clothes on a low stool. He turned for it, but the girl said 'Please!' again and took his arm.

Hood decided to play it as it came. He allowed himself to be led over to the fountain pool. They flipped the towel off and he stood there naked. He had had a good many experiences. But rolling naked in the snow in a Finnish Sauna or bathing in Japan had nothing on this.

The fair girl scooped water from the pool in a shell and poured it over him. It was agreeably fresh. The other girl had a sponge; they proceeded to bathe him and after the first minutes the whole thing became entirely natural. Hood gave himself up to a delightful moment. They moved round him gracefully, the girl with the blue eyes whispering occasionally to the other two. She was pretty – about nineteen, Hood guessed, with a firm-looking body and hair cut squarely round her face.

They towelled him dry, led him to the divan and Hood, stretched out naked, submitted again while they applied various mild-smelling balms and gently and expertly massaged him. It was prolonged and agreeable. When they had finished, he felt extraordinarily toned up and refreshed. The slight fatigue of the drive had vanished.

The fair girl was holding out a robe. Hood firmly intended to get back into his own clothes, said: 'No thanks,' and got up to cross over to them. But the clothes and stool were gone.

'Your things have been put in your room, sir,' the girl said. 'You must wear this when you see the Father.'

'The rule?' Hood said.

She nodded. 'Very well.' There seemed to be nothing for it. He stepped forward, put his arms into the sleeves and she helped him on with the robe and tied the belt. She looked very sweet, he thought. He caught a blush on her cheeks; but the next minute she looked away.

'What's your name?' Hood said.

'Malaren.'

'Like the lake?'

'Yes.'

'Pretty for a girl, the name of a lake.'

'Please come with me,' she said. She parted the curtains over the farther archway and led him through to a smaller room.

The fading evening light came through a single window. Hood took in the fine things – the lilac marble floor, a great red and gilt Chinese Buddha, nonchalantly resting one arm on a bent knee. Behind a silk-covered divan was a black lacquer screen which made Hood exclaim, and a Delanois chair worthy of a great collector. On a small table he saw a jasper perfume burner.

Zagora came in. Even in the big arch, he looked a giant. He was wearing a black robe, like an orthodox priest's, a long silver chain round his neck, and boots. His expression was one of sharp curiosity.

He came forward with a clumsy stride and at once

Hood remembered how Conder had said: 'He is a peasant.' His features were coarse, the nose too big, his long tangled hair reached to his shoulders. The skin was pleasantly tanned, the hands big and rough.

But his eyes made great effect. For a moment they were half hidden under his overhanging eyebrows. Then they showed – small light-brown eyes, mobile and disturbing, which seemed to be scrutinizing Hood's soul, ferreting out. Hood thought of the eyes of a mandrill, the hideous ape; there was keen intelligence behind Zagora's eyes, but the same animal ferocity. The next instant, their expression changed to something like benign understanding – and then again to shrewdness and cunning. Hood recognized the exceptional human being, a man of great magnetism – and probably of great evil. He felt the familiar chill of warning moments, the sense of impending violence.

'My son?' Zagora said. His eyes fixed Hood.

Hood saw that he was going to have to play things to the hilt. 'I bring you humble greetings from the Committee of Nine, Father,' he said. 'My name is Charles Hood. I'm an old friend of the Baroness Van der Goot's who has sent me. It is good of you to receive me.'

Zagora nodded. 'Are you anxious to receive the teaching?'

'Yes, Father, to know the enlightenment of the Way.'

'You have a communication to make to me?'

'No.'

Zagora stood absolutely still. Hood shrank inwardly but tried not to show it. Then, motioning Hood to a seat, Zagora stalked over to a table and took a custard apple from a bowl, ripped the top off with his teeth and gnawed. He tossed the broken fruit on to the table, wiped his hands on his chest, pacing down the room, speaking with his mouth full.

'You have troubles of the spirit, my son? You must liberate yourself, free your mind for the reception of the Great Universal Being. The enlightenment of the Way is through liberation, the casting off. The physical casting off of your clothes was symbolic. You have been anointed, as you shall be anointed in the greater freedom of your soul. He who knows the flesh and yet keeps to humility will become a valley that receives all the world into it. Being a valley of the world, with him eternal virtue will be complete.'

He stopped pacing, drew up a stool and sat down.

'Mystic phrases and parables – your pragmatic English mind, Mr Hood, has no taste for them, I dare say. You are English, Mr Hood, are you not? Yes, yes, it is unmistakable. I have the greatest admiration for the English race. There is a mystic touch to the English character which is hidden away and very difficult to reach and vanishes like breath on a wine-glass if one tries to touch it. This is one reason why my teaching is admirable for the Anglo-Saxon mind. Nowhere else is the concept of sin so admirably clear-cut and readily grasped. With the Latins it is muzzy and shifting, as so much else that is Latin. The English view of sin is deeper . . .'

The tone was slightly mocking. Hood sat fascinated. Zagora's small eyes bored into him as he went on with the monologue. Hood felt growing discomfort. The sense of danger had greatly intensified. He began to have the impression that Zagora was trying to hypnotize him. The compulsion of his personality was extraordinary. Hood felt a vague drowsiness. He took a grip on himself, shook his head, sat up.

Zagora's droning voice broke off. Hood got to his feet. He felt momentarily unsteady – punch-drunk – but made a great effort and threw it off. It had been a close thing. He said: 'I've always been told this is the time of the evening to see the mountains here.'

For a second more, Zagora was immobile, his curiously intent look fixed on Hood. Then he said: 'Yes. Let me show you.' He clapped his hands and the dried-up servant appeared, holding the curtain back.

They went out on to a patio with high vaulted ceiling and a double row of arches surrounding a long stone pool open to the sky. Cypresses and the multiple white arches were reflecting in the mirror of darkening water. Everything was beautifully designed. Statues and objects and books stood in the patio and the broad galleries between the double arches.

The place was deserted. Hood looked up to the ring of mountains beyond. They were smoky red and mauve in the dying sun. Overhead, the sky was already darkest blue-black. It was, he thought, a superb setting for so evil an enterprise.

The next moment he checked himself at the figure approaching between the arches. Zagora clapped his hands again. 'Balek! Balek!' The creature came up with long stiff strides – a man, Hood saw, but in appearance almost more bird than human.

Zagora was looking at Hood closely. Balek was over six feet tall, taller than Hood, his body and legs thin and almost rod-like with none of the form of muscles. The forehead receded rapidly with lank hair hanging straight back over it and, between the eyes, a great dark hooked horny protuberance emerged like a beak. The unblinking eyes were staring at Hood like a bird's. The skin was dark; there was a tiny mouth underneath the great beak. The man – if you could call it a man – wore a sort of smock and was barefoot. Hood was aghast.

'What is the matter, Mr Hood?' Zagora was saying. 'We have all seen men and women we thought looked like birds, have we not? Balek goes a little further. You may speak freely; he cannot understand.'

'What is that – that beak?'

'It is what the doctors call an osteoma, a bony tumour that grows on the face or head. They are so hard, these things, that they cannot be removed by surgery – but who would want to remove it? It makes Balek remarkable, does it not? I found him in New Guinea and of course it gave him great power there among his people.'

'It's appalling.'

'Come, Mr Hood; it is very ancient. Balek is of the greatest value and rarity. He is like Horus, the ancient

Egyptian god. He is the living proof that Horus – the god with the bird's head – was not legend. The ancient Egyptians of the first dynasties had seen a man like this. He had impressed their minds and conquered a position of power among them and so became deified. That is obvious. And Balek, just as Horus, has an affinity to birds. He is the most wonderful bird-tamer in the world.'

'Was that one of his vultures I saw as I came in?' Hood said.

Zagora swung round on him fiercely. Then with a visible effort he controlled himself. 'You have made a mistake, Mr Hood. Though vultures, of course, were known in the Dolomites centuries ago. I will show you.'

He turned towards the house. Balek remained silently where he was by the pool.

'You have not seen my Carpaccio, Mr Hood? There – it is a beauty, is it not?' He had led Hood up to a big Carpaccio canvas. 'A gift from the Committee of Nine. You did not know that?'

'It is very fine,' Hood said. He felt things were becoming hideously dangerous. The encounter with the creature Balek had not been fortuitous and he now believed that Zagora had been waiting for him and had prepared this reception. It was like going full-speed down a bob run you had never seen before, with no brakes.

'And there, you see, is a vulture,' Zagora said, pointing to the vulture in the landscape background of the picture. 'It was painted about 1501.'

'Yes. It's very fine.'

Zagora was moving away down the room, indicating that Hood should follow. They went out on to the terrace. The mountains facing this side of the house were already dark. 'So you will stay with us a while, Mr Hood? You will do me the pleasure of dining with me?'

'That will be a great pleasure.'

'Good.' Zagora clapped his hands and ordered drinks. The servant brought Hood an excellent martini, very dry and cold with a small green olive in it. Zagora drank raki. There was also a dish of mixed Japanese cocktail nuts which Hood had not tasted for years and which were very good.

He had said, as the servant appeared with these things, that he had never seen a Carpaccio sold and Zagora took this up and began talking fluently and expertly about pictures and the art market and collectors. And as they stood there in the cool evening with the drinks and the ring of mountains and the stars now out above, Hood felt the fascination of this other aspect of Zagora's character. The man who had been gross and monstrous a moment back had suddenly become extremely civilized. Hood no longer wondered that women were subjugated by him. Zagora conveyed a formidable resourcefulness, great force. The mysticism had receded and given way to sophistication – and yet it was lurking there.

'Bonnard – but Bonnard is the man to buy!' Zagora was saying. 'You will see, in a few years, Bonnard will be ranked among the very greatest painters of the century.' He broke off. 'Wait a minute, I have something that will entertain you.'

At his gesture, the servant who had been standing at a distance jumped forward. Zagora gave him an order and the man disappeared. In a moment he returned carrying a small picture and stood holding it up for them.

It was a picture of a chateau in snow, probably nineteenth-century French, Hood guessed. It was entirely conventional – and Zagora was not the man for such a lapse. Curious, Hood observed the thick frame. Then with a gasp he recognized it. He felt round the frame. There was a catch, the chateau scene folded back in two panels and there was the famous artistic titbit – Courbet's anatomical portrait of a woman's fig-leaf area.

In all its detail, done by a master hand, the portion that appealed to man's depravity gazed back at him. The 'portrait' was supposed to have gone to Hungary before the war and since to have been lost. Zagora was laughing. 'You remember its history? Courbet had painted it in 1866 for Khalil Bey, the Turkish rake and *viveur* of the Deuxième Empire. When it was done, there was a burlesque and drunken dinner-party at which Courbet and Khalil unveiled the thing as O – the Origin of the World.' He chuckled. 'But who was the model, Mr Hood?'

'I don't know,' Hood said. 'Courbet is supposed to have persuaded a lovely girl who had already sat for a nude for him, that he would immortalize her dearest attribute.'

'Sure enough he did. The only one immortalized!' Zagora's teeth gleamed. The small eyes were fixed on Hood. Inwardly Hood shuddered. Instead of humour, there was abruptly an icy chill in the moment. The whole effect was awful. Zagora looked like the force of evil itself.

Efim, the servant, appeared. Zagora said: 'Come, Mr Hood, we will dine.'

The big dining-room was ablaze with light. They sat at a long marble table, alone, served by Efim and three others. From the moment they began, Zagora ate and drank large quantities, cramming the food into his mouth with his fingers in Oriental fashion, spilling wine over the table and over his robe, wiping his fingers in his hair. He ate his own food, a sort of barley curry with much sauce. Hood ate mutton, which was well cooked. There were few exchanges, since Zagora was absorbed by the food. When he had finished the main dish, he ate a large quantity of fruit. Afterwards, he sat for a long moment observing Hood, then said: 'You are familiar with the doctrine of salvation through sin, Mr Hood?'

Hood thought he would do better not to admit ignorance. He said: 'Generally.'

Zagora's smooth manner of the terrace had returned. 'The idea of what sin is, of course, has shrunk so much in our day that the therapy itself has become less and less effective. Look at the seven deadly sins of antiquity: Envy, Gluttony, Pride, Vainglory, Avarice. Who, I ask you, Mr Hood, nowadays takes those seriously as sins? They are foibles, trifles, traits of character – scarcely worth noticing. They are rightly remembered, forgive me, as the moral furniture of the Victorian novel. Another, Pride, is actually well viewed in these modern times. And Anger – who would consider it sinful to fall into anger? The idea is comic.

'All these conceptions are out of date, Mr Hood. But there were originally eight deadly sins in the ancient world – and the remaining one still has a claim on us: Unchastity. The sexual life contains all the remaining sinfulness of man. Confession, of course, is a great liberating force, I will not deny — '

'So is destruction,' Hood said grimly.

'Ah yes. But it has been so cheapened, Mr Hood. True destructiveness is an art; but it has been practised by the vulgar. No, confession is finer. Sartre, of course, is wrong. Hell is not Other People; it is the Past. That's the attraction of confession! It is why it is so good to confess. But sex is finer than both of these.

'Sin in our time, what is left of sin, is inescapably bound up with sex. Freedom of the soul, its liberation for the reception of higher things, for communion with the universe is therefore freedom from the claims of sex. The ultimate release is sex. Don't you agree, Mr Hood?'

Once more, Zagora was scrutinizing him. 'No doubt,' Hood said.

'The principles I try to teach are simple. You will only break the bonds of your earthly attachment in the blessed exhaustion of all passion – when you have uprooted and destroyed the last vestiges of your bodily desires, cast down the last barriers to true humility and submitted yourself to the universal spirit.'

'And that is done — ?'

'Sin, my son. Through sin. Humiliate yourself through sin and you will attain the Universal Being.'

It was damnable – and at the same time, Hood thought, it was incredible that it could be taken seriously. Yet it had been, long before this, and its powerful appeal to any number of women was unquestionable. This was the teaching which Claymore had rightly said had done so much harm, had corrupted intelligent women who might have been expected to see through it or resist it.

Zagora poured his glass full of wine and drank with gorging impatience. A streamlet ran down his chin and Hood reflected that he seemed to enjoy this sort of gross behaviour. He put the glass down and called out something that Hood didn't understand to Efim.

'I feel sure you will be an apt follower of my teaching, Mr Hood.' He scraped back his chair. Hood was about to rise, but Zagora stopped him with a gesture. 'No – you are my guest. I am obliged to leave you, I have other obligations; but I wish all our amenities to be yours. All we have here is at your disposal. I invite you to think of whatever you have most yearned after in your secret self, most longed for – and indulge it. We can provide everything – anything!'

He was moving away from the table. Across the room Hood saw that Malaren had come in.

'You must rid yourself of the idea – I find it is a peculiarly rooted idea among some of my Anglo-Saxon friends – that women do not much like sex, do not enjoy it, and do not enjoy what are called deviations by the lawyers and um – other experts. But I feel you have not that mistaken notion, Mr Hood. In any event, I am sure you will find what you need here. You have a wide choice; the world was not made yesterday!

'Now you will excuse me. I have my hours of contemplation, my hours of penance to which I am bound. I am confident that you will make good use of our resources. We have gone to great care to make them perfect. You must feel free to practise anything you desire. Every facility is provided. Then we shall speak again. Meantime, Malaren will be your guide. Goodnight.'

Hood was on his feet, but before he could retain him, Zagora turned through the arch and went out. A current of air stirred through the room as if someone had opened an outside door. Hood was angry, baffled and repelled. Yet once more he felt extremely vulnerable. Malaren approached and stood waiting. Hood finished his wine.

Efim was hanging about on the other side of the room.

'Will you come with me, sir?' Malaren said.

Hood had himself under control. 'Sure, but first I want my cigarettes and my clothes. Will you take me to them, wherever that is?'

'The Master desires that you should do what he says, to prepare yourself further.'

'Let's do this first.' He looked straight at her. She hesitated then turned and led the way.

They went up a wide curving staircase, turned into a small loggia at the top and she opened a door. The room was austere; a low teak-framed mattress, a low lacquer table, reed mats. Beyond was a cubicle with shower and washbasin. No sign of his clothes. Then he saw the closet built flush with the wall and pulled it open. His clothes were inside – except the jacket.

He tapped the trousers pocket, found cigarettes and lighter. He lit a cigarette and took a deep drag. He snapped the closet shut and went to the door of the room. Malaren was just outside.

'Sin will have to wait, Malaren,' Hood said. 'You'd better get some sleep. See you in the morning.' He shut the door.

Hood sat on the bed smoking in the dark. He had put on his own clothes and found they had left his trouser-belt. This he only wore to use as an emergency weapon. The buckle was an ingenious piece of gadgetry which allowed the central pin to be snapped up and locked into place and when he wound the rest of the belt round his hand, he had a two-inch steel point in his fist. The moment when he would use it was rapidly approaching, he felt.

He was waiting. The house was silent. It was two o'clock. Out of the window, the moonlight showed up the surrounding lawns and threw masses of shadow here and there. He finished the cigarette slowly. Ideally, he should have rope-soled shoes; but his pair of lightweight calf were excellent.

He crossed to the door and eased it open. The loggia beyond was dark. He moved to go out, checked himself and hastily regained balance. Malaren was curled up naked on a pallet across the doorstep and as he looked down, preparing to step over her, she moved and sat up.

Hood put his fingers to his lips. She got silently to her feet, her eyes on him. Her body showed in the dim luminosity coming through the open door of the room.

'What are you doing here?' Hood whispered. 'I thought you were my guide, not my guard, Malaren.'

'This is my penance.' She did not seem put out by her nakedness and stood there quite simply, not trying to hide herself.

'What for?'

'I must fulfil my penances.'

'That's not a reason,' Hood whispered. He touched her arm. 'Good God, you're cold. Here—' He stepped back into the room, took the kimono he had worn earlier and put it on her. He folded back the sleeves and tightened the belt. It was far too big but better than nothing. 'Now you can go back to sleep.'

'What do you want, sir?' she said.

'A look at the amenities and a drink. Stay and guard the door till I get back, there's a good girl.'

'I must come with you.'

Hood looked at her. Pretty kid, all right, he thought. He said: 'Sure thing. You're the guide. Go ahead.' She led the way down the stairs, lifting the skirt of the kimono. Hood thought: I wonder if Zagora thinks I'd harm her? There must be something else. She's only his very frail first-line.

At the bottom of the stairs, the girl crossed the passage where a dim lamp was burning and headed diagonally through one of the large rooms giving on to it. As she reached the arch on the far side, Hood ducked back and raced tiptoe through the archway on the opposite side to which they had entered. He turned into the next room and found himself in a small lobby with only a glimmer of light through a closed shutter above. He stood still. He heard her pass, looking for him. He gave it a few minutes and stepped carefully out.

He went through the dim rooms, trying the shutters over the arched openings to the outside. But they were locked by some system that defeated him. He found two double doors, also locked, leading farther into the house and a brightly lighted passage shut off with an iron-bar door. He stood looking down the passage; but nobody appeared. There was obviously another part of the building from which he was cut off.

He went into the long narrow room next door and found a loose shutter. Cautiously he pushed it up and ducked out. He moved round in the shadow, scanning the area of the house which was inaccessible to him from inside; there was also, he found, another entrance. He scouted, searching for a way in; but nothing offered. He could see a glow from a skylight in the middle of the roof. Somebody in an inner room was awake.

Then faintly he heard somebody laughing. It was a woman. The laughter strengthened and continued, became uncontrolled. It was chilling. Hood shuddered. Was it Tiara?

There was a clink of gravel round the corner ahead of him. Hood froze against the wall. Another step sounded. He was certain somebody was going to appear. But nobody did. Yet it had been unmistakable. Somebody must be keeping sentinel on the other side. Hood moved back in the shadow, found the window and went in. He lowered the shutter, crossed the room and came face to face with Malaren.

'I lost you,' she said. 'I was frightened.'

'What were you frightened of?'

'Because I'd lost you. You ran away. Please do not go away.'

Hood said: 'Is that the valley of sin, down that lighted passage?'

She nodded. 'But I may not take you there now. It is too late.'

'That's fine by me. But how about that drink?'

'I will bring something.'

Hood went upstairs to the room and shortly afterwards she appeared with a bottle of grappa and a glass.

'Good girl.' It wasn't his favourite drink, but he was glad she hadn't gone for the raki. 'Come and sit down, Malaren. Get yourself a glass; no, take this glass and I'll have the tooth-glass.' She shut the door and sat on the bed. He poured the grappa and tipped it back and felt the hot ingot go down. She sipped hers, coughed and grimaced and put the glass down. 'Hurts your mouth!'

'That's the idea. You're not going far with sin.'

'No, sir.'

'Don't call me sir, Malaren.'

Hood looked at her in her innocence and sweetness – in this place. He felt sickened that she should be living so close to corruption and probably made to learn vile things. He lit a cigarette and poured another grappa. 'What would've happened if you'd really lost me tonight?'

'I'd have been punished.'

'The Master?'

She nodded. 'I would have deserved it.'

'That's not true. Drink your grappa. You need it; you were cold out there tonight. Why did you have to do penance?'

'I can't tell you, sir.'

'All right. But drink your grappa.' She took another tiny sip and coughed again and suddenly laughed. It transformed her face. 'That's the first time I've seen you laugh,' Hood said.

'Now shall I have a cigarette?'

'Debauchery.' He gave her one and lit it. After drawing she opened her mouth wide, letting smoke out of nose and mouth at once, coughing and rubbing her eyes. She handed it back. 'Horrible.'

'Oh, I agree.'

They sat together on the bed. Hood felt grateful to her. He shuddered at the thought of what the night would have been like in this place without her. She put a hand on his and Hood felt vaguely protective – a weakness, he told himself, and the cause of too many involvements. It would be too easy to make love to her; but she would not take it lightly and to hurt her would be damnable. 'How did you get here?' he said.

'I was sent by a lady of Odense. She said I must come and serve the Master. That is what I do.'

'Odense's in Denmark, isn't it?'

'Yes. Once she lived in Sweden. I was adopted by her.'

Hood said: 'Malaren, have you seen an English girl come here lately? Tall, fair girl?'

'I don't see many of them. I mean, there are many who come and I never know. Sometimes they come to this part of the house but more often they stay on the other side.'

Hood stubbed his cigarette, put her unsmoked one in his mouth and poured another drink. It wasn't bad grappa. He got up and went to the window. The moon was behind the mountain, throwing a mass of shadow on the ground. Now that he was here, he was going to have to adapt his course of action to circumstances, though he had hoped to discover more than he had so far. He came back to the bed. 'Listen, Malaren, I want you to get my coat. Do you think you can?'

She looked at him uneasily. 'No – I — It is in the other part of the house.'

'You could get it in the morning, couldn't you?'

She was silent and had become tense. Then she said quietly: 'All right. I'll try.'

'There should be a gun in it. Don't be alarmed. All I want is to get it back, if it has been taken. Do you think you could find out and get it back?'

She nodded resolutely.

'Don't you want some more grappa?'

She turned to him. 'No. I don't really care for it. Are you going away soon?'

'That I can't tell you.'

They sat quiet again for a while. She said: 'Did you ever go to Odense?'

'No. I was in Ringe, not far away. There is a fine light there. It's good for painting. It's a good town. Did you like Odense?'

'Oh yes,' the girl said. 'The lady who adopted me was not kind. But the town was very pleasant and there were many friendly people there.'

Hood said: 'Malaren, I have something more to ask you.' But he did not ask it immediately. She looked at him and said: 'Please, sir, ask me what you want. You can ask me anything.'

'You promised not to call me sir.'

'What do you ask then?'

'Do you know if there is always somebody on guard at the entrance gate here? I mean, that couple, do they ever go off for ten minutes or so?'

'Oh no; they are always there. Sometimes their son is too. They don't leave the gate for a minute.'

He looked at her. It sounded like something she had tested. 'Very well. Now is there any way into this place from the mountain side?'

She shook her head. 'There has been a rock fall – what do they call it? – a subsidence. It is very dangerous. Nobody goes there, even the climbers.'

'I see.'

Quietly she said: 'You want to come here without them seeing?'

He looked at her eagerly. 'Yes. Come on, my girl. How's it done?'

She didn't speak for a moment; then she said: 'There used to be a boy from the village. He was good-looking and a fine climber. They caught him in here one day. They said he wanted to steal, but I do not think he did. He wasn't a thief. Besides, he did not get into the house, only the grounds. But Balek caught him and he had an accident and was killed. They said he had fallen down the mountain while he was trying to climb and escape. His face was terribly torn and his chest had a hole in it.

They said it was caused by the sharp rocks.'

'Who did it – Balek?'

She nodded. 'They did not know how he got in. They never found out.'

'But you know?'

She nodded again. 'You go along the road outside the gate to the end of the wire fence. The fence has electric current through the top, so you mustn't touch the top strands. The end is fastened to the rock which overhangs the road just there and if you look up, above the fence, you will see an iron bracket fixed into the rock. It used to have a telephone line or an electric cable on it, the boy said; that disappeared long ago, but the old bracket is still there. If you can get a rope over it, you can climb and swing over the fence. You have to be strong and a good climber; but the boy did it several times.'

Hood gripped her arm. 'Malaren, you have the order of merit. That is obviously it!' He stood up. He was beginning to see the next steps. The first thing had been to penetrate the place – this visit could hardly be more than a reconnaissance. But now he had the clue to how he must proceed from here.

He went to the door and locked it. 'Now, my girl, I am going to sleep.' He started to undress. 'It's going to be daylight in a couple of hours and it's time we both turned in and kept each other warm. Come on.'

He stood before her naked. He bent forward and kissed her briefly. He felt her responding but gently broke away. She threw her kimono off and was quickly between the sheets.

Hood climbed in. She snuggled up to him. He could feel her mons veneris heating his backside like a warm iron.

'Goodnight, sweetheart,' Hood said.

'Goodnight, sir.'

CHAPTER SIX

HOOD WOKE up with a gentle touch on his arm. He opened one eye. A firm breast rested on his biceps. He contemplated it. He gave it a friendly joggle. Malaren was bending over him. 'You'd better wake up. I've brought you breakfast.' She was wearing her usual dress.

He sat up at once. 'Malaren, you're a treasure.' He felt ravenous. She lifted forward a tray with two fresh boiled eggs, crisp bread and a pot of coffee and put it on the low table. Zagora, of course, had to be equipped for this extremely good service and Hood realized that there must be a large staff in the place. He looked at his watch: 7.40.

Malaren went to the door, glanced out and shut it again. She came over to the bed but did not sit down. 'I am trying to find out about the English girl.'

'Any clue?'

'Any what?' She smiled broadly.

'Clue. Any indication she's here?'

'Do you always look like this when you wake up?'

'Like what, you little rat?'

'Your hair.' She laughed, then ruffled his hair with her hand. Her bosom jiggled enticingly.

Hood was exceedingly tempted – but killed the impulse. 'Did you find out anything?'

'Not yet. Drink your coffee while it's hot.'

He sliced an egg, lifted the top and dipped in. 'Where's the Master?'

'In meditation.' She began speaking of some ceremony for which Zagora was preparing. It sounded bogus and unrealistic in the bright sunlight, with the yellow of the egg steaming deliciously in front of him.

She went to the door again. 'I must leave you.'

He beckoned her back. 'What about my coat and gun?'

'Later.' She went out, shutting the door.

Hood finished the breakfast with relish. The sun was shining in a sapphire sky. He stood at the window, enjoying his first cigarette, looking out at the distant peaks which were now in a brown and grey mood. The air was so clear that there seemed to be no atmosphere. It presented a painter with the same problem as the Midi. Clear blue skies all the time – as boring in the end, he thought, as a clear blue life. But right now they were good.

He killed the half-smoked cigarette, went into the cubicle and stood under the shower. The water was soft and lathered the soap easily. He dried off and found a cordless Sunbeam in the drawer under the single shelf. Well, all right. He shaved, put on his own clothes and waited.

A motor lawn-mower was droning somewhere in the grounds. Once or twice he thought he heard women's voices. He lit another cigarette and mentally mapped out his action. The immediate thing to do, having seen this much, was to test Zagora's intentions – see whether he was willing to let him move in and out of the place. Zagora, he believed, suspected him, though possibly not why he had come. Hood had had to make this risky abrupt approach or the process of penetrating Zagora's circle would have taken far too long. It was a condition of the attack. He decided to play it straight and bland; go down, say he was going into the village to pick up a couple of things, get into the car – and see what happened. But he wanted his gun back first.

Malaren didn't reappear. He gave it another fifteen minutes, then went down. The shutters were raised, the french windows open and the rooms which had seemed so oppressive at night were full of fresh morning air and sun and he thought again how elegant the place was. Through the broad white arches he caught vistas of more arches, some, he now noticed, shut off by grilles. There was the pleasant lapping of a fountain. Nobody was about. Once more he had the feeling of being extremely exposed and had to check a compulsive desire to swing round.

He walked out of the house and stood looking round. The gatekeeper was slowly rolling the top of the stone pot which Zagora had thrown yesterday towards the terrace. He looked up and saw Hood.

'Buon giorno!' Hood sang out. The man gave no sign and bent over the pot again. An ugly bastard, Hood thought; his hair and eyebrows looked as if they were fighting a losing battle to stay apart. Hood noted his strength; he was moving the pot lazily, without effort.

Hood turned away and walked along the edge of the lawn. Somebody whistled behind him. He looked round and saw Balek at a fair distance. All at once, Balek spurted forward. He kept his arms stretched at his sides, touching his thighs, and covered the ground in stiff-legged strides, like a big bird running. Hood said 'Jesus!' under his breath. On the face of it, it was the most awkward possible gait – but as a dash from a standing start, he had never seen anything like it. He wondered what Roger Bannister, against whom he had run, would say.

Balek did not move into action and speed up. At one instant he was motionless, the next he was spurting. Then, just as suddenly, as Hood watched, Balek stopped for no apparent reason and stood turning his head in jerks as he looked round – a bird again. The speed, the strength, the extreme awareness were all amazing.

At that moment, Malaren came out of the house. Hood saw she had his jacket over one arm. The sense of immediate risk increased. Hood went to meet her. 'Good girl.' His hand felt the weight of the gun in the pocket. 'Any sign of the English girl?'

She shook her head. She looked scared.

'Trouble?' Hood said.

She nodded and in a whisper said: 'Careful! Please go quickly.'

'What's wrong?'

'They are going to kill you.'

Over her shoulder he saw Zagora come out of the house

eyeing them. Hood put the jacket on. He took his time. Things were now going to be unpleasant. He wondered if they had emptied the shells from the gun. 'Want to take a chance and come with me?'

She shook her head. 'I can't.'

Hood backed, keeping his eyes on Zagora. The change from the smooth reception of the evening before would have been amusing if it hadn't been sinister. There was no explanation – there didn't need to be. Zagora had simply been entertaining himself last night, sizing him up. Now the pleasantries were over.

Zagora advanced four paces and glanced at the gatekeeper. The gatekeeper moved slowly up the steps of the terrace.

Hood had no doubt now what was going to happen – but before he could react, Balek streaked across the grass behind the gatekeeper to a point level with Hood and stopped.

They were all watching Hood. Hood kept his eyes moving from one to another, at the same time surveying the ground for a breakaway. The gatekeeper stepped forward and from immobility, Balek gave another spurt. Hood saw it. Balek's bird-like speed had enabled them to fan. Balek was now almost outflanking him on one side and Zagora on the other. He had to snap his head full round from one side to the other to watch them both.

He tensed himself, back-stepped fast. Balek ran. Hood was as badly off as before and Zagora had closed. The situation was not good. He did not think he would be able to pull the gun fast enough to stop one of them getting behind him.

He fixed his eyes on the gatekeeper, keeping the other two in the corner of his field of vision, threw his hand inside his coat, at the same time backing as hard as he could. His gun covered Balek as Zagora moved in and the gatekeeper charged. The hammer clicked on the empty chamber – and on the next.

Hood flung to one side, feinted, swerved past Zagora, jumped clear of the gatekeeper's tackle and sprinted.

Balek was behind him. At that moment a bell sounded from the house.

Hood ran like mad, vaguely conscious of a commotion at the entrance gate ahead. The big gate was open and there were gesticulating figures. The bell was still ringing. A motor-cyclist in black leather coat, black breeches and helmet was inside the gate, straddling his machine.

Hood ran hard towards him across the grass, then realized that there was nobody after him. He threw a look over his shoulder. Balek was motionless on the lawn. The gatekeeper was farther back and Zagora had turned towards the house.

The bell stopped. It had been a signal from the gatehouse, he understood that much. Hood trotted the remaining distance to the gate and saw that the motorcyclist was a police road patrol, a *carabiniero*. He was signalling to something on the road outside – and as Hood came up, the stern of a big blue coach with 'Noble Tours' inscribed on it backed slowly in.

Hood wanted to shout exultantly. He looked up at the row of English faces inside – the mums, the men with open-necked shirts, two laughing ginger-haired girls at the back. Never had they looked so good. The woman gatekeeper was muttering savagely. Hood noticed her enormous mouth – a great cod-like gash. He went behind the coach and squeezed through between it and the wall. The tour guide, young and also ginger-haired, was standing at the entrance looking at a big Esso tanker blocking the road in the other direction.

'What's the trouble?' Hood said.

The guide looked round. 'Eh, this fellow here' – nodding at the tanker – 'coom oop the road and we couldn't get by. We rang the bell at the gate here and the bloody old dook wouldn't let us buck in, wouldn't orpen the gate. So we had to get t' bloody police. Lookily there was these two fellers joost down the road. They made 'em orpen oop.' Hood saw the second *carabiniero* on the road.

'We shouldn't have been oop here at all if there hadn't

been that diversion on t'other road. Road blocked; full o' stones or soomething.'

'Out from Lancashire?'

'Aye. Liverpool mostly. Coom down from Cortina this mornin'.'

'Could you give me a lift to Belluno?'

'Aye. Joomp in.'

'Thanks. Am I glad to see Liverpool!'

'Yeah! Yeah! Yeah!'

The coach dropped him in the main square, the Piazza dei Martiri. Hood stepped quickly under the arcade of shops. He went into the second, a chemist's, and bought a razor, soap, toothbrush and sunglasses. He did it slowly, watching the road, the square and the gardens through the door. There didn't seem to be any followers; yet.

'Prego,' the shopkeeper said. Hood nodded and went out. The square with its pastel-coloured façades and gardens was charming. But it was useless as cover. It simply wasn't busy enough. There were a few women shopping, cars pulling on to the car park opposite, children between the flowerbeds. Hood knew he was now going to have to move fast.

He stopped at the Café Matteoti and got the name of a shop which sold climbing gear; it was in the next street. Hood bought a flexible rope line, heavy enough for a hand grip, and a canvas bag. He went back to the arcade, found an outfitter's and bought himself a brown corduroy jacket, the nearest fit he could find, a pair of grey trousers and a terrible blue trilby hat in the style favoured locally. He put them all in the canvas bag, lit a cigarette and went out.

It was nearly eleven o'clock. He looked out across the square – the wide stretch of pavement, the lack of activity. Nothing for it. Carrying the bag, he walked briskly to the cinquecento arched gateway on the far side. Through the arch, he stepped behind the cover of a fruit stall and stood watching who followed. Three or four women came through, an old man with whiskers, a municipal official in uniform, then a short mahogany-faced man: a spotter for Zagora? Hood had to find somewhere to hole up for a few hours.

He worked his way through the clean bright sunny back street. A hotel sign said 'Grifone d'Oro'. He pushed open the narrow glass door. It looked perfect – small, clean and obscure. Inside was a tiled entrance, stairs up, dining-room opposite with plastic flowers and straight ahead, a low-ceilinged tiled café room in old-fashioned style with corner counter, tables and espresso machine. A tall Modigliani woman of about thirty-five with a long neck came out smiling. Yes, she could give him a room.

It was a large double room with wallpaper, light wood furniture, white bedspreads, pleated paper light shades and gave on to a small square. Hood looked out. There were two empty parked cars. No watchers.

He took out his gun and checked it. It was his Colt Cobra, empty but in order. Zagora had obviously never intended him having it back and had simply emptied it as a supplementary precaution. Hood had brought the Cobra, which was half an ounce heavier than his favourite Agent, because it would take ·32 or ·38 New Police Calibre shells or ·38 Specials. But was he going to find any of these in Belluno?

He undid the parcel and changed his clothes. The new trousers were short. He did what he could and transferred the belt. He rang the bell and ordered a grappa. A tall young man, obviously the son of the house, said: 'In the salle downstairs, signor.'

'Send it up here.'

'Prego.'

When it came, Hood took the drink to the window. He stood at an angle looking out. He was going to have to go back to Zagora's in daylight – at the latest dusk. He couldn't take a chance on the climb in the dark. He did not relish the expedition. It was going to be difficult to approach the place without being seen. And if he found Tiara there, it was going to be dicey getting her away.

No fun at all. But that, after all, was the object of the exercise.

Hood knew he had in the meantime to keep off the streets; but one errand he must accomplish first. He finished the drink, put the hat on and went downstairs. On the floor below, a priest was coming out of a room, shutting the door behind him. Hood noticed that he was sweating profusely. It made him glance at the room number: 15. Downstairs, two other priests were sitting at a table in the dining-room at early lunch.

Hood turned into the street, walked rapidly downhill to the first café. He asked for a telephone book, looked up gunsmith in the trade section and mentally noted the single address. The man behind the bar told him the way. It was nerve-racking to saunter, looking casual.

The shop was shut. Idly, Hood rattled the door handle as if it didn't matter much. Nobody answered. Silently cursing, he went down the alley alongside and almost passed the side door with the name plate and *Armaiuolo* – armourer. An elderly oval-faced man in a leather apron answered the bell. He looked at Hood over his gold-rimmed glasses. Hood explained what he wanted. He did not show the gun. The man shook his head. 'No, no. I have not got any, signor. I have shot-guns, one or two shot-guns, sporting guns....'

'Thanks.' Hood turned away. 'Buon giorno, signor.'

'Wait a minute, though. I am thinking ... Come in.' He shuffled into the shop which was darkened by the arcade outside. Hood watched the street through the window while the man searched interminably, saying: 'I am thinking...' and at last produced a box. He wiped the dust off. There were some loose ·22 shells and three ·38s in it.

'Ecco. It is all I have,' the old man said. Hood took the ·38s gratefully.

He walked back to the Grifone d'Oro. The priests were still in the dining-room eating and had been joined by the sweaty-faced one from room 15. A lot of noise was coming from the low-ceilinged room beyond and Hood saw that it was now half full of men, all talking. He stood looking them over. They were local men, weatherbeaten and mostly middle-aged, all sitting in their hats, talking a lot, chivvying each other and laughing and drinking. They drank red wine. A girl of about fifteen was doling the wine out from big dark blue quart bottles – Hood thought of medicine bottles – that she held by the top of the short neck. With the casualness of infinite practice, she filled the glasses to the brim and never spilled a drop.

Hood went in and sat down. When the girl came up, he nodded to the bottle. She poured him a glass full. The wine was thin and not good. Hood sat with his hat on facing an advertisement for Cinzano painted on a narrow mirror. Nobody took any notice. Four of the men were playing a game with the long narrow Venetian playing cards. Hood watched the street door in the mirror. He had no trust in Belluno.

Gradually the salle emptied. As he got up, the priests came out of the dining-room ahead. They stood talking for a minute in the entrance, then they went out together.

The thing clicked in Hood's mind. He snapped his fingers. Of course! In Italy the *priest* was the invisible man. He saw what he was going to do. As he passed the table where the card-players had sat, he took a couple of cards off the top of the pack and pocketed them. He went up to his own room, left the door ajar, lit a cigarette and stood listening. He finished the cigarette unhurriedly and went to the landing below. He turned along the corridor to room 15 and stood outside listening, then knocked. If anybody answered, he was looking for an imaginary Signor Borgoni.

Hood felt the tingle of excitement. Nobody answered. He tried the door but, as he expected, it did not open. He took one of the playing cards from his pocket, inserted it between the edge of the door and the frame and let it drop until it stopped against the hasp of the lock. This was the old burglar technique, originally done with a strip of celluloid, known as 'loiding' – but also equally feasible with a playing card or a 'Please Do Not Disturb' sign, the hotel thief's classic tool. It would only work if the lock wasn't turned.

Taking the two corners, he worked the card up and down. The card slid lower. It was behind the hasp. Hood gave a twist. The door edge swung out. He took it with his finger-tips, opened it and went in.

It was a double room with the priest's belongings placed neatly, a notebook on one bedside table, a pair of big black shoes, framed snapshots, suitcases. Hood shut the door behind him and stepped to the wardrobe. There was a starched white vestment on a hanger and a soutane. He took the soutane, reached into his pocket and tucked a ten-thousand lire note under the hanger. He searched for a hat but couldn't find one; a beret was hanging on a hook behind the door and he took that.

As he turned the door handle, somebody came along the corridor outside and stopped. Hood eased the door shut. He heard a key clink on its ring. He flattened behind the door. The key rattled in a lock farther down and the next moment a door slammed. Hood went out.

He shut the door of his room and tried on the soutane. It was generally too small; he took a razor-blade and let down the hems on the skirt and sleeves and judged it would pass. The beret was fine. He reckoned that once he got to Mas, the walk up to Zagora's place would take him about an hour.

He stretched out on the bed to wait. The square outside seemed to be a favourite short cut for the Belluno traffic. Scooters tore the afternoon air. How was it that people like the Italians who were supposed to be sensitive to music could stand so much noise in their daily lives?

The image of Malaren nagged at his mind. He hoped Zagora hadn't taken it out on her. The sound of the woman laughing in the night returned to him. Laughing death. What was the connection between this and Diana Undermere?

The patch of sunlight crept across the floor of the

room. He looked at his watch. Half past three. It was time. He found himself grappling with reluctance. Damn it, the thing had to be done. He got up, put the rope in the canvas bag and wrapped the soutane and the beret in the paper from the outfitter's. He took the bag and the packet and went down into the lavatory on the half-landing above the entrance. He put on the soutane and beret, gripped the bag and shot the bolt.

Down the half-flight of stairs, he turned into the entrance with head averted and was out in the street. He had thirty yards to go to the taxi rank at the entrance to the Piazza dei Martiri. He climbed into the first. 'Go up to Mas.'

The taximan turned as if he were puzzled by Hood's accent. Hood said: 'Presto! Presto!' The man muttered something and they drove off.

Out of town the roads were empty. They took the fork for Agordo. At Mas, Hood paid the taxi off and walked on towards the last houses. He could feel the taximan's eyes boring into his back. Damn it! an unlucky start. He swung along the high road. He walked steadily and unhurriedly. He tried to trudge, in the way a waiter or a priest does, men who are professionally on their feet all day. The undulating stretches of grass at the roadside were still green. The sun was declining. There wasn't a breath of wind – blessing of the Dolomites.

Normally, Hood would have enjoyed the exercise, the clear air, the clear light. But the loneliness of the road now was threatening and oppressed him. A car came up behind and he bent to tie his shoe-lace, keeping his head down until it passed. He took the narrow upper road and passed the gate walking silently on the grass verge. The road was deserted, the sun dropping towards the mountain peak. It was an hour that often made Hood shrink with irrational fear. At the end of the fence he at once saw the bracket, a rusty arm nearly three feet long with a short upright, sticking out well above the top of the fence. Two feet inside the fence, at about the same height, there was a tough-looking root emerging from a crevice in the rock. Hood stood looking from one to the other. It was quite plain; he understood the method.

He rounded the bend immediately ahead and scanned the road. It was deserted. Zipping the canvas bag, he took out the rope line and tied a running loop. He threw it. It missed and fell with a thud. He threw three times more without success. At the fifth shot, the loop caught. He hauled it tight.

Hood whipped off the beret and the soutane, stuffed them in the bag and tossed it over the far edge. He watched the bag tumble under a bush. Perfect. He transferred the gun to his trousers pocket, went back and spat on his palms. He jumped, grabbed the rope and went up hand over hand. He reached the bracket and hooked an arm over.

Trees hid the house from view. He hauled the rest of the rope up, threw a loop over the root; then, gripping the rope with both hands and steadying himself against the rock wall, he let himself swing in and over. It was easy. He went down the rope and dropped to the ground.

CHAPTER SEVEN

THE SUN was behind the mountain claw. Hood went fast through the shrubs and trees till he saw the house. There were lights on and he could see figures moving about. He scanned the grounds for Balek. The rolling expanse of green round the house, now slashed by the great wedge of shadow from the mountain, was empty. He searched the line of trees on his right; nothing, Inwardly he recoiled. By God! but it was a damned sinister place though.

He followed the fence under cover of the shrubs until he was level with the house. Then he sprinted across and flattened against the wall. It was a small porch with a glass roof. He edged in and opened the door facing him.

Dingy stairs led up. Servants' entrance. The door on the landing above was locked. Hood followed the stairs up and out on to the roof.

He took his bearings. He was above the area of the house from which he had been cut off earlier. Mingled voices came up from below. He tiptoed to the edge of the roof and looked over.

A group of about fifteen women were sitting on low seats and cushions below talking with Zagora in the middle with trolleys of drinks standing round and four or five servants moving about or waiting to be summoned. Some of the women were young and most of them wore kimonos and sandals and manifestly not much else. Low necklines showed their figures. They all looked very chic and swagger and cared-for with their smart hair-dos and jewellery – and Hood thought it was exactly the sort of tone he had imagined. They were all crawling to Zagora. They were all enormously conscious of him. They were besieging him – rich maladjusted women, most of them refugees from a mundane world which had failed to give them satisfaction, refugees from the disillusion of life, from failure to find a God, from unsatisfactory husbands and the limitations of materialism, yearners, all of them, for some superhuman experience which would restore a meaning to their existence and give them the secret. Zagora was a god-substitute. His manner seemed to be deliberately crude. He looked at some of them with insulting frankness, interrupted, laughed coarsely, shut them up with a gesture. Yet whoever he spoke to, the woman was obviously dominated.

It was obvious that Zagora's strangeness – his crudeness and contrast with the culture of the other world they moved in – was his strength. Hood could see exactly how he would use that. Women of this sort needed to be dominated. But if one of these disciples ever turned under his insults, Zagora would explain that his affronts were meant to provoke them to resist, to become independent – and thus aware of themselves. They would fall for that. Numbers of other women had done so already with fashionable gurus of the day.

But in despair, Hood saw that Tiara wasn't there.

A pretty young blonde moved over and sat down next to Zagora. He shrugged at something she said. The next moment she idly flipped open her kimono, showing her long legs. She had nothing on. Zagora glancingly appraised her, spoke a word or two and turned to one of the others. They ignored the girl, competing ruthlessly for his attention. Whatever 'the ceremony' had been, it was apparently over.

Hood crouched there. He knew he was in great danger and that he had to take no account of that.

Another girl came out under the colonnade, a tall brunette in a flimsy transparent robe and a little silver-coloured turban. The others took her in, trying not to seem to. She was extremely beautiful with great poise. She went to the edge of the pool opposite Zagora, deliberately undid the girdle of her robe, let it fall open, then shrugged it negligently off her shoulders. She was naked. Her large firm breasts swayed gently with her movements. She let the robe slip away and Hood caught a sort of quiet gasp from the other women, immediately followed by a louder burst of conversation as they tried to pretend it was of no consequence. Then, catching up the robe again, the girl half covered herself and walked round to where Zagora sat. Gracefully, she slipped into the water, swam a short distance and lay floating. The water moulded the flimsy robe to her figure emphasizing her voluptuousness.

Zagora was watching her with approval. He extended a hand in her direction. She came to the edge and lifted herself out with a quick movement, the robe clinging to her. Zagora's teeth gleamed.

All round, the mountains were blazing in the sunset, the colours changing in delicate modulations – a rose flush, a red blaze with undertones of blue, pale ochre and then rose blending into ash.

Hood shrank. Somewhere a woman had begun to

laugh. A few of the others looked up uneasily. Hood couldn't see who it was; the laughter became louder and a woman came out of the house. She was about forty, in a smart brown suit. She walked unsteadily, the laughter shaking her; then she seemed to have a bout of shivering.

Before she could reach him, Zagora jumped up, stepped over the women round him and went to her. He took her hands. She stood laughing in his face, swaying and shivering. Zagora's eyes were fixed on hers. Hood was stone. Somebody else in the group behind began to giggle, then broke off. The woman's laughter was dying away. It stopped. Zagora led her back into the house.

At that moment, Hood saw a figure moving in from the descending gloom of the lawn beyond. It was Balek. He moved in short jerks, not running but turning his head from side to side. He seemed to Hood to have sensed his presence.

Hood backed off. A light was shining through the skylight of a room below. Cautiously he looked in. It was a high-ceilinged room with light walls. There was a divan to one side and Tiara was lying on it. She stirred, putting her arm under her head, staring into nowhere. Her kimono had fallen open, showing her midriff and her legs.

Hood felt the shock go into his belly like a low punch. He said 'Christ!' to himself, gritting his teeth with mingled relief, anger and tension. His heart was thudding and he thought she had never looked so extremely glamorous. Was she here of her own choice, on an escapade? He thought she couldn't be. But everything was going to be a damned sight worse if she were.

He looked round. There was a hinged glass roof-flap fifteen feet away. He found it was fastened from below. He worked on it, gripping the flap and forcing it back. He could feel the fastening underneath bending but it didn't give.

The light was going. He cast round in desperation for some implement. He picked up a sliver of bone – something left by the vulture? – and found that he could touch the end of the fastening with it. In a moment the flap came free and he heard the fastening fall below. He crouched down, not moving. Nothing happened.

He lifted the flap and looked down into a passage, swung in and dropped. He turned right in the direction of the room with the fanlight and pulled his gun. The first door was open. As he went in, Tiara jumped up from the divan and screamed.

'Shut up!' Hood shut the door and faced her. 'Move fast. Get your clothes.'

She was staring at him, momentarily petrified. He stepped up to her, standing stock-still looking back at her searchingly. 'Did you come here of your own accord?'

'No – no —'

'Get moving! We've got a few minutes to get clear.'

'Charles ... Oh God.' She broke into movement, casting about confusedly. 'What's happened? Where is —?'

'Save it. Where are your things? Shoes and a dress.'

She ran to a wall cupboard and reached in. She dropped the kimono to the floor and stood naked and the next moment with raised arms, was wriggling a dress over her head. Ear to the door, Hood saw her pull on a pair of shoes and start looking for something else.

He jumped to her side, grabbed her arm. He caught her scent and for a few seconds stood looking down at her eyes and her lips – the little bitch; marvellous girl, all the glamour in the world. He said grimly: 'Lady Evenly, you have just two things to do. Keep your mouth shut and keep your nerve. Do you understand?'

She looked extremely frightened and just nodded. Gripping her arm, he moved to the door, opened it a crack. From somewhere below there were voices. The passage was empty. She was fumbling with the open front of her dress. He turned along to the section under the open fanlight, put the gun in his pocket.

'When you get up there, don't move.' He jerked his head upward, then bent, grabbed her ankles and lifted. She put her arms on the edge and hoisted herself through.

Hood raced on tiptoe down the passage and grabbed the two chairs against the wall. He put them back to back under the fanlight, whipped off his tie and lashed them together, stepped up, judged the balance, then did a quick step-up on the joined backs and sprang upwards. His elbow was on the edge; he hauled himself through.

'Duck down!' His whisper was urgent. She was standing upright. The light was sinking to dusk but he had a mortal fear of Balek seeing them. Crouching down, he led the way to the service staircase. As they reached it, there was a cry, a long tearing sound like a night-bird's, from the park beyond. She clutched his arm. Balek! He pulled the gun. They headed down the stairs.

Below, he pinned her close to the wall of the house with his free arm. The grass was greying and once again Hood caught the atmosphere of menace. High above, the mountain-top was a dying purple, fading to ashen grey. He spoke in a whisper. 'We have to cross separately. When I tell you, run for those shrubs – straight and hard. Keep your head down. Ready?'

'Wait.' She slipped her shoes off, took them in her hand, wriggled her skirt up over her knees to mid-thigh, then nodded.

'Go!'

She ran out into the open, holding her skirt, her head bent forward. Gun ready, Hood watched the corner of the house. His shoulder muscles knotted with tension, dread of seeing Balek streak across the grass after her. Halfway across, clear in the open, she stumbled.

Hood's jaw clenched. She kept her balance and a moment after reached the bushes. He fixed the spot and bent down, waiting. Then he leapt forward. He sprinted full out. In the cover of the shrubs, he flung himself down and swung round scanning the grounds. He could see some of the servants moving about beyond the corner of the house where Zagora and the women were.

'Tiara!'

She came through the shrubbery on hands and knees. He took her by the shoulders and kissed her. She was shivering a little. Her lips were cold. She crawled up against him. 'Oh Charles, I'm so scared. How are we going to get out?'

Hood knew they weren't going to make it by the rope.

'By the gate, kid.' He tried to make it sound confident. 'Keep your nerve. Come on.' He dived into the shrubbery.

The cover was good along the fence and they followed it down. Then, about ten yards from the gatehouse, Hood stopped. He put his lips close to her ear and spoke in a whisper.

'Keep back here under cover. Don't move until I call for you. If there's some rough stuff, don't look. If we're unlucky, you'll have to run back. Okay?'

She nodded. He dare not use the gun; it would bring Balek out or might give one of them in the gatehouse time to ring the alarm bell. Gripping it by the barrel, he crept forward and crouched under cover of the shrubs. He rapped the gun butt against the stone corner of the arch. The light from the gatekeeper's lodge was shining under the archway. Nothing happened.

Hood rapped two or three times again and scraped the butt along the stone. He crouched down waiting. Still nothing. Then a segment of light brightened. Somebody came out.

Whoever it was, was standing still, listening. Hood's searching hand found a stone. He judged the distance, tossed the stone carefully. It landed at the corner of the arch and didn't rebound. A shadow moved. The watcher was stealthy. Hood waited, crouching in the dusk. The figure of the gatekeeper came slowly out from the archway, searching the edge of the shrubbery.

Hood was hardly breathing. His eyes were on the man. The man stood looking cautiously round. Then he relaxed and straightened, as if he had decided that it was merely some small animal after all, and turned his back.

Hood sprang. The long Colt butt caught the man's head with a crunch. He staggered, his knees buckled a bit. Hood's arm was round his neck, dragging him back into the shrubbery; for a few seconds the man went slack, legs limp, checking Hood's movement, then with a mighty heave, he pushed up from the ground, his elbow swinging hard into Hood's liver. He twisted free. Hood dropped the gun deliberately and dived on the man.

They crashed down. Hood got a locked strangle across his throat to stop him calling out, but the man kept jabbing awkwardly with his knee and elbow for Hood's crutch. He was very strong and much the weightier. He tried for a finger-snap hold on Hood's right hand and as Hood broke, caught Hood with a hard heel-kick to the knee.

Hood straightened up. The man ducked to a crouch, arms wide to catch Hood's legs – and rushed. Hood blocked the rush with bent arms. His left hand gripped the man's shoulder, his right passed under the lowered head and, as the man drove in, he linked arms with a wrist-lock. The man's head was jammed under his right armpit. The man tried to twist free, punching out for Hood's crutch again. Hood gritted his teeth, knowing what was coming – and gave the neck a violent snap up. There was a muffled crunch. Reluctantly, Hood held on as the man's body went into a prolonged and sickening quiver, then flopped. Hood dropped him on his face.

He crouched down. The bastard's kick on the knee hurt. He saw Tiara move just behind and she came out. She was white but under control.

'Charles — ' she said breathlessly. 'Are you all right?' Her eyes went to the man's body.

'Keep back. There's somebody else.' He searched round and found the gun. He hesitated, then put it in his pocket.

From the ground behind they heard the cry again. It couldn't be long before somebody found that Tiara was missing. Perhaps they had already.

Hood's mouth was cindery. The whole place filled him with nausea. He crept nearer to the gateway. Everything was quiet. He could see faint shadows shifting across the reflected light from the gatehouse as the occupant moved about. Hook took off his belt, snapped the pin upright and locked it. He slipped the belt between his two middle fingers, just below the buckle and pin, wound the rest round his hand and gripped the end.

A small sound came from the gatehouse. A shadow stretched upward. Then there was the silence of someone listening. A woman's voice called out. Behind him he heard Tiara catch her breath.

Again there was dead silence. Hook wanted desperately to scan the grounds towards the house but dare not. A step padded softly under the arch. Was she coming out? Hood prayed she had not heard the fight and rung the bell to the house. He threw a glance back over the sweep of grass and dark trees – and as he turned back, saw the woman two feet away in front of him. She was lifting her eyes from her husband's inert form. In the second's delay, Hood saw how tall and knotted she was, saw her register fear and then her great slit mouth open in crazy fury. He rose and as he stepped towards her, she threw herself on him.

Her arms gripped his throat and she took his weight with a turn of the body, keeping his belt-hand up with her bony, high-pushing elbow. Hood broke her grip, but she stumbled and fell unexpectedly, clinging to him and bringing him down and the next moment, her enormous mouth fastened on his throat.

Hood strained away in horror. She was gnawing at him. She was wiry and hard as bone. He struck at her but her arm took the blows. Blood was running down his neck. She was making slobbering sounds, working her fish-jaws in mucus and blood, trying for his jugular.

Hood clutched at her hair, wrenching her head back. Her teeth clung to him, lifting him with her. He felt himself on the brink of passing out. Wildly his hand jabbed the steel belt-pin into her arm. He reached round her head with his other arm, caught his fingers in the corner of her mouth and dragged her free of his throat.

As she flung off she spat at him, writhed free with furious eel-like twists. He scrabbled up. She threw a kick at him and in a flash he turned sideways, caught her heel in the crook of his right arm, yanked it high and at the same moment crashed down his full weight with his other arm just above her knee.

She screamed as the joint broke. He threw up the leg still higher, kicked away her supporting leg and as she fell, flipped her over and jumped on her spine. She made a vague swimming motion with her arms. The bloody mouth sprang open like a dead cod's. She lay still.

Hood was trying to control his tremor. He touched the blood and slobber on his neck and the gnawed skin. Holding his handkerchief to it, he stood with hanging head for a moment, then, as Tiara came up, he snapped out of it. She gave a frightened exclamation and clutched his arm. He buckled his belt on.

'The gate!' They ran under the arch. The door of the lodge was open, the smell of something burning in a saucepan came out and Hood felt a shudder at the incongruity of this homely touch and the fight he had just gone through with the housewife. He went in. There was a small panel of six buttons, one black and five white. None of them was marked. Hand to neck, Hood hung over the panel, then turned searching. *How did they open the gate?*

'For God's sake, try to find the button,' he called to her. They searched with a sort of wild despair, finding nothing, no indication. Nor could they identify the button that rang the alarm.

Tiara was biting her lip, searching through the two neat rooms with the burning smell coming out of the kitchen beyond. Hood hurried outside and hauled vainly on the great gates, then tried to follow the electric wiring from gate to lodge. It was no good. At any moment, Balek was going to appear under the arch.

He ran back to the lodge and stepped across to the panel. 'One of these bloody things springs the gate. This is the gatekeeper's lodge and logically they'd be using the gate button more than any others. It ought to be this one.' He touched the black button. She nodded. Hood said: 'Get ready to run,' and pressed the button. A red eye lit up at the top of the panel. Nothing else happened.

Tiara turned to him in frantic fear: 'It's the alarm. We've rung the alarm bell!'

'Hold it.' Hood was icy. He pressed the button below the black and they heard the click of the gate springing open. 'Come on! Run like hell.'

They dashed out through the gate on to the dark road. Hood grabbed her arm, hurrying her on. He steered her down the road for fifty yards, then said: 'Over the edge. Dig your heels in. Hang on to me. If you hear 'em above, keep still.'

He pitched over the verge, turning his feet and digging the welts and heels into the grass, feeling her clinging to his coat. The slope was covered with grass, trees and sparse bramble, and was fairly steep but not impossible. They slithered down in the dark, then on a steeper incline he slipped and went crashing twenty feet into a bush. Pain throbbed in his neck. He heard her gasp with fright above. He called up softly: 'Take it easy. Come on down.' He had to wait till she negotiated the steeper part and slipped into his arms.

There were muffled voices above. 'Keep going, kid,' Hood said. 'We've got to make the road below.' They stumbled and slid down, striking patches of bare earth and stone and having to go round until they found grass again. When he urged her on she gasped: 'Darling, I can't go any quicker!'

Abruptly he gripped her arm and stopped. Lights were showing above and two torches shining down from the roadway. He could see other figures moving near by. 'Get down!' Hood whispered. The voices were clearer. Two of the figures ran along the road. The torch carriers were flashing their lights along the grass and trees near the edge. Hood prayed the traces of their descent weren't too visible. Then one of the torches moved over the edge. 'They're coming,' Hood said. 'Let's go.'

The torch went out but he could hear the movements

above. The next moment he slipped and went sliding down, dragging her with him. Branches whipped his face. then as his hip hit rock, his coat was briefly caught by something. He threw out an arm, grasped a root and held on. His other arm still held the girl. He could not get a purchase with his feet on the smooth slab of rock. She was scrabbling to get hold, hanging by his arm. The sounds above momentarily stopped, then came on, as if the searcher had direction. Hood's feet scraped vainly. The searcher was approaching.

'Don't move,' Hood's voice was a whisper.

He hung on, craning up to try to see through the dark tangle of grass and bramble and trees behind. He could feel the blood running down from his neck inside his shirt. His right arm gripping the root had his own full weight and Tiara's. He gritted his teeth with the effort to hang on. He felt his grip weakening.

He strained his head back against the rock, jamming his elbow in among the big tangle of roots he could feel to get support. The power of his fingers was going. They hung there in the dark and Hood knew he was going to let go. The searcher above seemed to be turning away. Hood's jaw came forward in a jutting grimace. A moment more of agony. Then he let go.

For a few fleeting seconds, his jammed elbow took the weight, then Tiara swung away, they dropped. It was fast and steep. Then they were both sprawling against a grass hump. Hood lay still, recovering. The dim shape of her face was turned towards him. The grass and branches of the pines were rustling above. They didn't move. The rustling retreated.

'Close thing,' Hood said.

They crouched while he worked the circulation back into his arm.

'Charles, look – they've got a car!'

Above them, the beam of a car headlights was probing the grass slope and the patches of bramble. Zagora had sent a car back along the road and was running it close to the edge as a searchlight. Hood saw they had to reach the road below before another car pinned them. 'Come on!'

They clambered and slid down and reached the road. 'Into the ditch.' It was hardly two feet deep but dry, and they ran crouching along it. For the moment the road behind them was dark. The enemy were searching in the opposite direction, which meant a swoop down where they were next.

As if she had guessed this, Tiara clung to him. The faint luminosity from the sky showed the line of her cheek and neck. He said: 'You're doing all right.' He turned and moved on faster. A thick clump of pines loomed out of the dark ahead. As Hood headed for it, they heard a car in the rear.

They ran for the cover. Hood pulled her down beside him and crouched, looking back. The car was approaching down the loop of road above, stopping at intervals as the occupants got out to search. There were three men, Hood saw; one, at least, with a gun.

His took her arm. His voice was as casual as he could make it. 'We're going to get the whole pack of them along here in a minute, sweetheart. If you dodge them, get down to Venice and find Arthur Graff. Remember; Arthur Graff. He'll take care of everything. Okay?'

She threw her arms round him. 'I'm not going without you – I can't—'

He held her with cold anger away from him '*Okay?*'

She shrank and nodded. He looked back at the car. It was nearer, now coming down the straight incline towards them. It stopped once again and the men dived into the darkness.

Hood said: 'We have to get that car.'

'No ... oh God.'

'Stay here.' He went through the trees towards the road for a moment, then came back. He cast round in the low tangled undergrowth, bent quickly and straightened up holding a strip of broken carton. He faced the girl. His voice was harsh and urgent. 'Listen to me. We have one chance and you have to get it fast. I want you to cross the road now and flatten out opposite. There's a pile of wood or something. Get behind that. I'm going to stop the car. When you see the men get out, you do one simple thing. You pick up some stones and throw them *behind* the car, make 'em think we're back there. Throw them one at a time at the trees or at the road so that they'll hear them. One at a time. Then when I wave my hand in the headlight, come out and jump in. Understand?'

'Charles, don't leave me.'

Between his teeth, Hood rapped out: *'Do you understand?'*

'Yes.'

'Then do as I tell you!'

Her fingers were digging into his arm. He took her to the roadside. They saw the car still stopped farther up. The men were making very little noise. Hood hoped grimly that they had seen what had happened to the gatekeepers. It wouldn't help their self-assurance.

She hitched up her tight skirt. 'Now!' She ran across the dark road. He turned quickly into the trees, knelt down and bent the strip of carton to an L. He stood it up, took out his lighter and flicked it alight, then adjusted the flame and stood it, burning, in the shelter of the carton.

He moved away fast through the trees for a short distance, then bobbed down into the ditch. The men returned to the car and started coming down again.

The masked glow of the lighter showed faintly through the trees – smaller than he'd imagined. The car came nearer, moving slowly as the men scanned. Hood tensed. Then they saw the glimmer, snapped off the headlights and cut the motor and came coasting down in silence. Hood peered through the darkness. He held his breath. Now he couldn't see them. He had a moment of panic, believing they were close on him. He heard the faint click of a door. He guessed they had stopped and were getting out of the car. Dimly he made out two figures silently crossing the grass verge – but no third. *No third.* Where was the third man – in the car?

Hood crept forward a few feet. The car had stopped in the deep shadow of the trees and it was hardly distinguishable. He could not hear a sound from the men. Abruptly the lighter in the trees went out. He did not think they could have reached the spot yet. He groaned inwardly – then saw that it would make them think they had been heard and the light doused.

He edged nearer the car. They hadn't much more time. Why in God's name wasn't Tiara throwing the stones to draw them off? But he realized then that she must barely be able to see the car's position, if at all. He gritted his teeth. If this kept up, he would have to tackle the car blindly. With Number Three there somewhere out of sight, it would not be good.

A twig snapped in the undergrowth beyond. He tensed – then he could have shouted. No twig – a stone. It was Tiara! Another stone came down. He strained into the dark. Black moved on black – somebody going stealthily towards the area behind the car.

Hood crept in another yard. A stone fell on the road badly short, then another, near the car. Now she was lobbing them too close in! Another minute and the men were going to realize the thing was a trick.

Hood moved silently along the grass verge to the car. His hand ran along the wing, touched the door. He inched his head up to get a sight inside. The car was empty. He pulled his gun, held it in his left hand, and took the door handle. A stone dropped well to the rear, like a snapped twig again. There was a faint exclamation from the dark and he saw a figure move. That's the girl! he rejoiced.

He eased the door open. The car was a low-slung Lancia. Hood crouched, his eyes searching the opposite verge. He dared not call her and they couldn't wait. She *must* be watching the car! He reached inside, cupped his hand round the roof light and quickly snapped the button on and off.

Nothing happened. *Come on, Tiara, come over.* He

implored her mentally in the dark. He signalled again, rapidly on-off. Somebody moved in the undergrowth beyond. One of them was coming back.

In desperation, he eased himself into the driving seat. His mind mapped the sequence of action; slip the gear, flash with lights, start, veer to opposite side, throw door open – and *pray* – pray she could jump before they started shooting. He opened the other door, touched the key – saw her running in across the road.

He pushed the door wide. She was in, breathing hard, ducking protectively. 'Don't slam it – hold it,' he whispered. He released the hand-brake. Slowly the car began to roll forward with the incline. Then he threw in the engine, trod down and they were leaping away and the men behind shouting. There was the crash of shots and a bullet slammed on the coachwork. Hood was straining to see the road and yelling with relief as they went fast downhill.

'Baby – we made it! We made it! My diamond Tiara baby, we made it!'

She was sobbing and laughing at the same time. 'I thought I should never see you there in the dark. My God, how awful...'

'Grab a cigarette, in my pocket. Give me one and sit tight. They've got cars and we're not out of it yet.'

He was tempted to switch on the lights to improve their speed but decided against it.

'No matches,' she said.

'Hell, I forgot. Doesn't matter.'

'Charles, they have people down in —'

'Baby, I love you but talk later.' He was driving as fast as he could on the dark unfamiliar road. The surface was bad. Nothing showed in the mirror behind. His eyes were grim and narrowed. A few kilometres on, he braked and flashed his lights at a sign ahead. *Deviamento 500 metri*. 'What's this?' He couldn't remember noticing any deviation on the way up; but why should he, coming the other way? Then his eye dropped to the red blinker on the dashboard. Petrol: empty.

'Hell!' he said under his breath. Tiara had seen it too. 'That fluke shot – got the petrol tank.'

They were going to be dry any minute. Hood's jaw set as he hunched at the wheel. Dare not use the lights now. At the curve below they took the deviation on a narrow road which rose over a hump, then headed out over an open area of hillside. Hood scanned it in dismay. He couldn't see a sign of cover or a light. Dimly white, the unsurfaced road curved into the gloom. The dark extent of open country around, sloping gently away to the right, offered nothing. High up the slope on the left he could see a dark mass of rock like a tower.

They ran on. The road dipped and the right-hand slope fell sharply away. Below, in a hollow, Hood made out a single isolated clump of pines. He swung the car to the edge, backed and pulled round at right-angles.

'End of the ride, sweetheart.' They jumped out. Hood released the brake and pushed. The car went over and pitched down the grass slope, missed the first trees, then hit a stone, veered and came to a stop partly concealed.

'Come on.' They struck off across the opposite side of the road up the slope, stumbling and running.

Hood glanced back. The pursuing cars were much nearer, turning in at the deviation.

CHAPTER EIGHT

THE GOING was over grass at first, and easy. Then the slope became stiffer and strewn with stones. Tiara kept up but they didn't make a great pace. Hood held her arm, catching her up when her shoes twisted on the uneven ground.

The cars dipped briefly out of sight on the far side of the hump, then topped it in a dazzling glare and came on. The second car had a mobile light and they were swinging it to search the areas on either side of the road.

Hood and Tiara ran on up the slope, paused for breath and ran on again. The pinnacles of rock loomed above them in the dark. Tiara pitched forward again and he shot out his arm to save her from falling. He held her, giving her a breathing space. She looked up at him, gasping, painfully breathless but game, couldn't speak, and he turned to look down at the cars below, gritted his teeth and said, feeling a monster: 'Sweetheart, we have to go on.'

They stumbled up among the stones. Hood could see a small outcrop of rock a hundred yards on and was forcing her on to it before the cars reached the dip where they had ditched the Lancia. She tripped, swung on his arm and nearly went down. He picked her up and ran with her like a child in his arms and they reached the outcrop and leant back against it with thudding hearts.

Hood looked around the edge, quickly drew back. The sound of tyres moving over loose stones came up. She pressed against him. The second car was a jeep and was moving up, sweeping the slope with its light. Hood drew her farther back behind the rock. There was a crevice about a foot wide and they squeezed into it, hearing the stones snapping out under the jeep's tyres. It looked as if Zagora's men had found the Lancia.

The dark blazed and headlights swept over the slope beyond and came round full on the rocks. Hood crammed his fingers down for his gun. The headlights were steady, showing the texture of the rock and the litter of stones and Hood had the incongruous flash of a Chirico canvas. A man's voice spoke briefly. Then the lights swung away and Hood was blinking blue, trying to see, as the rubbery snapping of stones retreated.

They eased out. The jeep was pulling on to the road below and turning away. The other car was already at a distance.

'Come on.' She said nothing – he had half expected her to joke but she was too scared – and they went on up the slope again. Farther up they struck another narrow track which intermittently faded out and reappeared. It was a marked path with slashes of white paint on the rocks. They followed it round. Hood kept her going, hauling her on when she wanted to stop.

Ahead, by the path, they saw a hut.

'Darling, please – can't we stop a bit,' she said. 'I'm out.'

'If it's empty; we'll see.'

The hut was isolated and as far as he could see offered no cover for a quick retreat. When Zagora located the ditched car, he would be back scouring the area. But they had covered a good distance and had to hide up somewhere.

It was a two-storey wood and stone club hut – Hood made out a sign on the doorpost. He went round vainly hauling on the heavy shutters and kicking the door. He shouldered the door – but that was hopeless. She was sitting looking pretty exhausted but still game. The single first-floor window at one end hadn't been shuttered. Hood picked up a big stone.

'Will you try that?'

She nodded, got up, wriggled her skirt over her knees. She climbed on to his shoulders, broke the glass, opened the window. A moment later she had climbed in.

Hood turned, scanning the darkness. A few lights twinkled in the distance – of Belluno or what, he couldn't tell. Closer in, red lights glowed on a pylon and there were many more farther off. Nothing seemed to be moving in the expanse before him. Bolts rattled and he went round to the door.

'Oh, Mr Royce,' she cracked bravely, 'I was thinking what a boring evening it was going to be with none of my drinking friends dropping in.' He saw she was trying to play off the tension and recover some of the poise that had been so violently destroyed in the last hour or so.

It was pitch dark in the hut. He was mechanically searching his pockets for his lighter, then remembered.

They hunted about for a light, bumping into invisible furniture, brushing each other's faces with extended hands. She called out from a corner: 'Wait a minute, getting warm. Here's a gas-ring or something.' The next minute she was rattling matches.

'Hold it!' Hood said. He stumbled, knocked something over, cursed and slammed the door. 'Okay.' The match flared and the room emerged – a long rough table, chairs, wooden steps leading up, climbing gear hanging from nails, antlers over a dust-dimmed glass. With two more matches, Hood went up the steps and shut the shutter over the broken window above. Then they found a hurricane lamp and stood in the dim glow looking round while she pushed her hair back from her face with the back of her hand.

She took a step towards him. She put her head against his chest. She was biting her lip to stop herself crying from relief of the tension. She put her arms round him.

'Are they coming back?'

'Probably. We're all right here for the time being.'

'Those two at the gate – it was terrible.'

'It was going to be you and me otherwise.'

'Don't, don't.'

'How did you get here? And why did you give me the slip at Gaston's?'

'How did you know I was here?'

'Answer me!'

'Oh Charles, it isn't the moment – don't be rough, don't bully me. Surely you can see – I was just amusing myself to begin with. He is an extraordinary man, fascinating, many-sided, attractive in that odd way—'

'We can skip that.'

'I thought you were asking me.' She looked reproachful and unprotected (playing the game, he thought). 'I was flattered and pleased. I could tell you of a hundred – five hundred smart women who are dying for the chance to know him, simply to meet him for half an hour and be able to say so, to get on the fringe of that circle of his, let alone be – well, pursued by him.'

'He'd been pursuing you?'

'Of course. I was fooling. Then, when I left you that morning, I drove to a big house he had borrowed from one of his women near Loches – a great rich place – and things began to go wrong. He was furious because I hadn't brought Tickle with me.'

'What!'

'Oh, he'd asked me before. He'd kept saying he wanted the two of us to join some party of his and he specifically wanted her to come on this occasion. I asked Tickle – it was amusing – and we'd arranged everything. She was coming. But then at the last minute she put it off, said no – she had something else on, I don't know what – so I went alone; and when I turned up at Loches without her, he was exceedingly angry. I'd never seen him like that before. He wanted me to call Tickle over urgently. He kept on insisting and I very nearly did, but then I said I couldn't, it was silly.'

'Why, suddenly?'

'I didn't like the tone everything was taking. I told him so. I told him I couldn't, quite frankly, and that I was going back home. Then he became awful – a monster. They locked me up, gave me some drug – I don't know how it was done – and I found myself here, in that place there.' Gradually, as she told this, she had paled.

'They tried to kidnap Tickle in London.'

'Oh God!' She was instantly tense again. 'I knew that! I knew something was happening. Is she all right?'

'As far as I know.'

'Charles, how *do* you know all these things? How is it — ?' She broke off, watching him as he lit a cigarette and took a deep hungry drag. He told her briefly.

'Charles Hood?' she said. 'It's much better than — '

'Tiara, listen!' Impatiently he interrupted. 'The thing of supreme importance is this: has Zagora been trying to make you give those ICC notations, formulae, data and so forth?'

'Oh yes.' She looked nervously away, then back at him. 'Yes.'

'Have you given any?'

She shook her head.

'Positive?'

'Altogether. He has this strange compulsion . . . several times he's had me on the very edge – almost like when I'm working with Tickle and the thing comes up from nowhere, just appears. It's been like that, nearly there – I confess I've hardly been able to resist and perhaps in another day or two I would have said something; but I have *not*, Charles. I have not!'

'Good girl.'

'He has also been trying to get me to make some mental communication to Tickle to come out here or to Venice, telling me to think of it, to concentrate on it – to get it across to her to come.'

'Sure.' Hood nodded. 'The thing now is to get clear of this place. It's no good moving before the morning.'

'Charles, you're hurt. We must do something for your neck.'

It was throbbing like hell. 'In a minute.' Hood stooped, trying to get the lamp to burn a little brighter but it remained dim and wouldn't respond. He straightened up. 'I could eat a horse.'

'Perhaps there's some tinned *charcuterie chevaline* – or some pemmican.'

'That old Nokomis stuff?'

'Listen, Pau-Puk-Keewis, if that's not good enough — '

He grinned at her. That was better. She was recovering. He said: 'Let's find out what goes on here.'

The hut was a single room with a gallery above around two sides where more climbing equipment, camping gear and a good deal of general junk was stored. One corner below had a gas-ring attached to a butane bottle not yet empty. They found two tins of ravioli, a tin of tomatoes and a small quantity of water in three of the camper's water-bottles hanging on the wall. She put the food on to cook.

'Domestic!' She looked up at him and he felt all the old signs; it looked as if he were going to be caught for another interlude of rapture and torment – if they got away alive. They held each other in a long kiss and she wound her arms round him with passion and tenderness and when they broke, she put her forehead against his chest in the gesture that had given him a pang before. She unbuttoned his shirt and put her hand inside and pressed herself close. Then she disengaged herself and, defensively, as if she had to counter the tender moment with some hard little crack, she said: 'Now I have to get back to training – you know, my next Olympic mile.'

'You qualified for the hurdles as well.'

She was quick and served up the hot food on tin plates from the camping gear and as he came in from a brief scout outside, she said: 'Look what I found.' It was a half bottle of Hennessy VSOP. 'But you'll have to drink it straight or have brandy and cooking water.'

The food seemed like the first Hood had tasted for a week. She talked light-heartedly, trying again, Hood saw, to counter her uneasiness. She asked him about his life and Hood told her some things. But when he wanted to know about Zagora and the activities at Kuan-t'eng and the women who came there, she said: 'Darling, can't we go over all that later? I feel they're so close. They have an oppressive sort of hold over you. If we start talking about them now they'll suddenly creep up on us. I'm sure of it. I want to get away from them for good. Please understand, will you?'

He looked at her, hesitating. 'All right.' He poured two drinks and she drank hers with a little shudder.

'Cold?' He remembered she had nothing on but the light dress and got up to look for something among the stacked gear in the hut. 'This damned lamp!' The light was going and when he tried winding up the wick again there was no improvement. 'Out of oil. We'd better get installed.'

He hauled over two sleeping-bags and was spreading them on the floor when she said: 'Twin bags, darling?' and laughed.

'We'd better.'

'You can't say you never make love on duty. I've proved it.'

'That was for a purpose.'

'What! Are you trying out the proposition that you made love to me simply as a chore?'

'No. But we may have to make a quick exit tonight.'

'Darling, you know how it is – easy come, easy go.' Another laugh.

'Go to bed,' Hood said.

'But a sleeping-bag's been one of my places ever since I read *For Whom the Bell Tolls*. Why shouldn't it toll for me?'

He laughed. 'You have a gift for the single entendre, sweetheart.'

She kicked off her shoes, wriggled her dress up and peeled it off. Hood felt the punch as he looked at her. She didn't need to strike a pose – those long legs, the smooth hard thighs and the breasts with lift plenty of women never saw again after twenty. She was one of the lucky ones who look slim when they're dressed and who undress to advantage. So many slim women had boyish hips when they took off their clothes and were much less appetizing. Tiara had slimness and shape. He went over and kissed her. She held him hard. 'Charles ... be nice. Make love to me.'

'Won't do right now, sweetheart.'

'Long time no fun. What do you want me to do to you?'

She was gently exploring.

'What are you doing?'

'Consumer research.'

'Go to bed,' Hood said again.

'Let's have some nature studies.'

'Your homework will have to wait.' He held her firmly away from himself and then watched while she got reluctantly into the sleeping-bag. The lamp was going fast now. He got out of his clothes, put the gun beside him and slipped into the other sleeping-bag.

He lit his last cigarette but one. She was close to him.

'That looks a very old bag you've got there, darling.' She laughed again.

'Shut up.'

'No man is an island – or shouldn't be.'

'Go to sleep.'

'That girl of Hemingway's was lucky, at least she'd been raped.'

No answer.

'You've been saying "Come on" to me all day. Now you come over here on the target range. Charles ... darling.... A gal has her rights after all....' She made a feline purr that all at once conjured up overpoweringly the night at Gaston's and conveyed her special glamour. It was irresistible. Hood stubbed out the cigarette on the floor and climbed out. He laid the gun beside the other bag and climbed in. The lamp went out. Her warm body was against him.

'Love in the dark – suburban! Don't you feel tigerish?' she said, laughing. 'Darling – bring your revolver in with us. It's what they call Lithuanian roulette – so exciting!'

The light of morning showed round the shutters. Hood stirred. Her creamy back was curved against him, but she was awake. She had been awake for ten minutes, silently inviting him. She moved her derrière fractionally again. His arm went round her and found the warm curves. She was wonderful. Damn it, no! It was time they cleared out. She caught his hand as he was drawing away and pulled him against her. She wriggled her derrière. 'Darling ... h'm ... ?'

Hood reached outside and zipped the bag. She yelped in protest. But he pulled her to her feet. She put her arms round him again. 'Charles, I'm burning for you at both ends! One more – a heavenly one, like that, just now ...'

He kissed her. 'It'll have to wait, honey.'

They dressed. She started to hunt round for coffee, saying there must be some in the hut, but they couldn't find any more water in the bottles and, anyway, Hood was anxious to move.

'We're going to try to get along the valley,' he said. 'Avoid Belluno entirely and go up the Piave for Feltre or even to Primilano if we have to. Then, once we're south through the mountains, we can strike for Vicenza or Padua. The thing is to get a car.'

He left her in the hut while he scouted outside.

It was a fresh morning with a light mist. There was nobody in sight on the surrounding slopes. They wedged the door of the hut shut and struck along the path between the marked rocks. It led over a rough hillside and then divided up – obviously a climber's route – and down.

They went downhill, soon struck grass and in half an hour more reached a surfaced road. There were muddy wheel-tracks and at intervals in the grass verge, deep scores filled with water – all obviously the marks of heavyweight traffic. As they went on, one side of the road fell away in a dizzying drop and they were going down sharp bends with the inner side rising in a steep rock cliff.

Hood felt uncomfortable. He wanted to get off this section of road. He wished they had found another route. There was no possible concealment or room for a breakaway. Ahead the road curved down out of sight. Tiara started to sing a naughty version of 'Miss Otis Regrets' as they went down.

Nothing passed them for fifteen minutes. Then Hood saw a car swinging up the curves below. It was a black Fiat, moving slowly and turned out of sight for a moment, then reappeared coming up. As it approached it accelerated. Hood saw a black dress and a peasant's shiny black straw hat alongside the driver and a heavyweight man behind. Locals? He signalled, but the car did not stop. He followed it round, wondering where it was headed. They weren't climbers, at any rate.

He turned back. Tiara had stopped singing. Her face was dead white.

'What's wrong?'

'That was them. That woman, I saw her there.'

'Are you sure?'

'Absolutely.' The car had disappeared.

'We have to get off this damned road.' They began to run. The surface of the road was ridged with mud indented by the tyres of heavy vehicles. Hood searched for a way down, any descent from the road. But the tops of the pines were standing just below and the drop was sheer. The inner side of the road had been built into a stone wall against erosion. At the next bend, he found a gulley on the outer side and a couple of small trees within reach. He put a leg over, gripped the grass and knelt.

'Darling – I couldn't make it,' she said. He knew it was too steep. They ran down to the next curve round a shoulder of the descent and Hood gave a shout.

The hillside was cut away in a vast excavation which stretched far back with pump tubing, parked lorries and scattered draglines, excavators, grabs and earth-moving machines. It looked like the early stage of a big hydro-electric project – the area was thick with them – and to Hood it was sweet.

He looked back up the road. No sign of the black Fiat yet.

'Tiara, sweetheart – *run*!' She went as hard as she could and they were twenty yards from the entrance to the excavation area when Hood saw the jeep swinging fast up the loops below. It was moving at speed; must have been a signal from the Fiat.

'Quick!' She slipped on the heavy mud and he grabbed her. He hauled her splashing with him through the stony puddles, slithering in the ruts churned up by the lorries and machines.

'Hy! Yahoo!' he was shouting. Why was there nobody here? Why was it deserted? He was yelling at the top of his voice – for a watchman, drivers, anybody; and then realizing with sudden grim despair that it was Sunday. Sunday!

For an instant he pulled up with the shock, staring at the prefab engineers' huts, locked and shuttered, even the smaller unpainted hut, supposedly the watchman's, with the door shut, the bulldozers and cranes and grabs idle. Presumably the watchmen were only absent temporarily; but he couldn't wait for them to come back! There was nobody else.

Suddenly Tiara began to laugh. Hood froze. It was like the woman's laughter, racking and unhumorous, that he had heard coming from Zagora's house. 'Tiara! What's the matter?'

She seemed to make an effort and checked herself.

Hood sprang into action. He hauled on Tiara's arm and splashed over to a gigantic dump truck, as big as a tank, parked by the nearest hut. 'Say good-bye to your dress. Lie flat! Only chance.' He lifted her to pitch her over the edge; but the truck was too high. Carrying her, he ran to another near by and heaved her up and she fell in with a clang.

'Keep down!' he yelled. He flung away, pulling his gun. The jeep surged into view, slithered round in the mud and four men jumped out.

There was one thought in Hood's mind – to draw them away from the truck. Tiara might, with luck, get away. He ran as he had never run. The mud, the fearful ruts, the great pools of water, the sudden humps and plunges were murderous going. His spine jolted painfully as he went down an abrupt drop. One of the men began shooting. The solid thud of sound made Hood gasp.

He ducked, twisted, swerved, running for the far side of the excavation, counting the shots as they came. Two! He swung behind another truck as two more shots in quick succession slugged into the bonnet. Four! There seemed to be only one of them shooting. He dropped under cover of the great quadrupled rear wheels and looked back. Three of them were spreading; the fourth, crouching by the jeep, had a rifle.

Hood lifted his own gun in his hand. The range for a pistol was hopeless, especially with his short-barrelled Colt, meant for close work. But he wanted to show them he was armed. He braced himself against the tyre and brought his left hand up for a two-handed target grip. Films often showed frightened women shooting in this style – yet the grip was an expert's, far more accurate than the conventional off-hand. Palm vertical, his left hand closed over his right already gripping the butt. The left-hand fingers rested solidly under the trigger guard, forming a support, taking all the weight of the gun and leaving the right hand for squeezing. For fast shooting with this grip, Hood used a refinement, cocking with his left thumb instead of his right. He sighted and squeezed. A miss – but not by too much. The man by the jeep ducked! Hood could not afford another shot yet.

There was a punk then hissing as a shot slammed into the truck's front tyre. One of the others, moving to outflank him, must have a gun too.

Hood broke into the open, running for the side again. Out of the corner of his eye he saw the black Fiat pull up and the doors flung open. The next minute, he was floundering up to his calves in mud and water, the innocent-looking puddle unexpectedly deep. He hauled himself out, went crashing down as his foot caught a hidden tangle of wire.

His arms flung out. He clung instinctively to his gun but felt it dig hard into the mud – and he was up and running again. He reached the cover of a pile of trench sheathing. Another man was running for a flanking movement on his left. The others were advancing, spreading out, under cover of trucks and humps of earth. He couldn't spot Zagora or Balek. Grimly he looked at his gun. The barrel was choked with yellow mud and gravel. He dare not fire it; it would be asking for a barrel-burst. He thrust it back into his pocket, gauging the distance he had to cover to the far side.

He could see a narrow cutting which would give him some protection as he scaled to the top. His jaw was set. He didn't give himself much chance of getting up there. He got on his marks. His eyes narrowed as he searched the chaotic expanse of mud and torn earth ahead for the danger points, the hollows he could use for momentary cover. Excavators, grabs and earth strippers were scattered over the area. But it would be a mistake to hide behind them while the enemy advanced.

He got set. He was breathing steadily, flexed, in control of himself. He knew that the run ahead was going to be the run of his life and that he did not have the odds on his side. He had faced this sort of situation before. But, he recognized, it had never been with quite the same finality. He had done his damnedest; and if this was how it had to end – he would see them all in hell.

He burst out and raced like mad for the cutting. He made his long stride, his eyes desperately charting the uneven ground ahead. He sprang up piles of earth, pulling free of clinging mud – terrified of losing a shoe. A shot whanged past his head. He swerved, leapt a puddle and, above his own hard breathing, heard a shout from the man in the rear.

He zigzagged erratically, expecting more shots from the rifle; but nothing came. He skirted a crane and ran in line with it over a good hard stretch, then skidded and careered wildly in loose mud, trying to recover balance. He fell, got up again. His shoes and trousers were gorged with mud. Then he was trudging and dragging along and the dream he sometimes had in bad periods, in which he tried to lift leaden feet to run from some imminent danger, had become reality.

Why weren't they shooting? The side of the excavation was still appallingly distant. In front of him was a mound of loose earth, and he had the shattering vision of a trench on the other side which he would be unable to jump.

He sprang up the mound. No trench! The surface was treacherously shifting. There was a hiss behind him and a shadow swung overhead. Something clanked heavily and he looked up as a gigantic steel claw swooped on him. He flung himself aside. It missed him by a foot. It tore into the earth, scooped some up, paused, then jerked again, spilling the earth out and, with a hiss, swung down in another murderous grab. They were grabbing at him with a 60-ton excavator! The claw-edged scoop thudded into the earth two feet away.

Hood sank knee-deep into a hole, gasping. The arm of the machine was lifted overhead. He could see one of Zagora's men working the levers in the cabin beyond. The grab was working an over-arm action with a wrist-like snatch at the end. If the bucket-scoop hit him it would tear his body in two without pausing in its motion. If it caught him between the manganese claws it would pluck off an arm or leg like a boy pulling off the legs of a fly.

The piston thrust out the machine's extension arm. Hood wrestled his mud-heavy leg free, threw himself backwards as the claw smashed down, biting deep, making the earth shudder. The driver had thrown in the hydraulic ram action – trying to swat him!

Hood was on his feet and moving away. The machine had creeper tracks and followed. He must try to get out of range. He slugged across the mound and down the far side. The claw came down just behind him. A moment later, as he looked back, he saw the driver jump out but couldn't see where he ran.

Hood dropped on one knee and hung there with mouth open and chest heaving. He looked up and saw that in the effort to avoid the excavator, he had unwittingly changed direction. The cut he had been making for was farther off! He thought despair was going to overcome him, make him give up. Blood smeared the back of his hand when it touched his neck. The wound was bleeding.

Hood didn't know how much longer he would be able to go on. He clung to the tiny respite as if he were in the ring, gaining every second after a knockdown, listening to the count, clinging above all to that distant muzzy '... six ... seven ... eight ...' through the roar of the crowd and the blasting of his ears. '... Nine!' He jumped up, running once more, straining forward.

Now they had brought the jeep into the chase. He could hear it behind him. He splashed across a wide puddle, feeling his pace flagging. The going was even more cruel here in this area where rock was being stripped and torn out. There were waves of broken rock between the great machines and the stretches of churned earth.

The jeep had pulled up. They couldn't continue with it. A tiny hope began to glow in Hood's mind. He turned his head to see what was happening, tripped and fell. He felt the warm painful glow of a wrenched ankle, but got up quickly on one knee. Then he saw the bucket of a rock shovel dipping on its boom above him.

Hood was stock-still for one instant in appalled fascination. The steel bucket was about twenty feet up. It jerked to a stop as if the driver didn't know the controls, then tipped sharply and slid out on its dipper-sticks towards Hood. The bottom of the bucket dropped open like a great lip and with a gasp Hood heaved himself away as it dipped down to eat him.

He clambered over the broken incline. The shovel clanked after him, hissed and the bucket dipped towards him again like the mouth of a prehistoric monster. He twisted, changed direction. He could hear the steel lip clashing and clanging against the bottom of the bucket as it opened and shut behind him.

His windpipe was rasping. The whole 80-ton shovel was moving on creeper tracks, stretching its Neanderthal neck for him. He twisted yet again, jumping down from the rocks and scrambling up a sticky earth slope.

Hood knew he was rapidly reaching the end. He had fought to the limit often enough to know how much strength he had in reserve – and now there were no breathing spaces between the rounds and he couldn't take a count. In a moment he would check his movement, trying to catch his breath, be unable to move in time – and the steel mouth would snatch him up. The ignominy of such a death would make it no easier to accept. The machine would crunch his body like celluloid, chew him, spit him out on to the gashed earth and then bury his pulped and minced remnants with a few manipulations of the levers.

Hood pulled up, chest heaving, and looked round. He had an instant of cold clarity. Every second seemed detached from the one that followed, though everything happened with great celerity.

He saw that there was no escape. The driver was manoeuvring the shovel towards him. He could see two of Zagora's men beyond and three more with the jeep. Behind him was the slope of rock and sticky earth which he could not climb fast enough to get away. Two or three more dips with the shovel and it would be all over.

Just below him was a huge drag-shovel with bucket hanging in mid-air. Hood put out everything – ran with all his remaining strength towards it. The enemy shovel-mouth came for him. He swerved. He ran ... ran ... sprang over the last rumbled rock and jumped for the ladder and swung up into the cabin. His heart was banging sickeningly and he could hardly see. He wanted to throw himself down, to give himself over entirely to the gasping need for breath and gain a tiny space of time in which to recover; but he couldn't. He staggered against the side of the cabin, dropped to his knees, somehow got up.

There was a leather seat in front of a bank of round-knobbed control levers and foot pedals, more levers and switches to the left. A window gave a view forward; above was a skylight.

He hauled the sliding door to and flopped into the seat. Half-blind with sweat, he saw the other shovel moving towards him, the heavy-duty bucket with its four projecting teeth hunting like the under-teeth of a great snout. He slammed at switch after switch – nothing happened. He had no idea how to work the machine.

He saw the small electric-control box overhead, threw a switch painted red and the big diesel engine throbbed into life. The black knobs of eight levers stared back at him. Hood was gripped by paralysis. Which lever to pull? How in God could he unleash this terrific power without knowing how to control it?

He sat gasping for breath, his sodden trouser-legs clinging to him, his shoes, swollen to enormous size with mud, slithering on the pedals. Then he trod down, slipped off, yanked blindly on one of the levers. The cabin slewed madly. With a mighty crash the 40-foot steel boom hit the bucket of the other shovel as it came up. Hood's cabin rocked. The enemy snout stopped and swung away.

Hood could not bring the lever back into position; he was vainly trying to find the right pedal-lever combination. He clung to the levers, longing for respite. He saw the steel shovel-snout driving in and there was a shuddering clang, Hood nearly went off his seat as the teeth caught the underside of Hood's dipper arm.

Hood stamped on the pedals, hauled a side-lever and gasped as the boom of his shovel soared aloft and stopped with a jolt that shook the whole machine. He knew he was at a disadvantage. The enemy was a stripper shovel which worked a tremendous dig-lift action, was tons heavier and had a long reach. But his own drag-shovel with its overarm downward-clawing action carried a mighty smash. A Triceratops versus a Tyrannosaurus!

He *had* to get the top joint of his neck, carrying the toothed bucket, extended.

The enemy shovel was manoeuvring in, lowering snout for an attack. Hood's bucket-head reared and smashed down on it. There was a grinding crash, the teeth interlocked. The enemy's bottom lip fell open and clanged as if the monster was bellowing in agony.

Hood's cabin was shaking so much he half rose, then realized that the enemy was retracting its double dipper-sticks, drawing its bucket inward, an action he couldn't counter. He pulled the levers. His bucket wrenched free, soared and crashed down on the two cable sheaves at the top of the enemy's boom. The enemy's lip clanged in pain.

Hood worked the levers, trying to repeat the smash,

made some mistake and sent his bucket into the ground with a crunch. The next minute he looked up and saw the enemy shovel was holding a great rock in its teeth. The bucket rose higher, began to swivel. It was going to tip the rock on him, crush the cabin.

Hood concentrated on the controls, pulled a lever. His boom rose, crashed into the shovel's extended bucket; the rock lurched and fell out. With a grind like a snarl, the shovel dropped its neck and trapped Hood's bucket-head. They clanged together. Hood managed to get free and smashed down. The gigantic necks tangled again. Hood had begun to understand the controls.

He could not see Zagora's other men. They were on the far side of the machine. He had the idea of attacking them with the shovel; but they had at least one man with a rifle. All he could hope for was to disable the enemy shovel and get enough respite to break and run for it again.

There was a blistering roar from the right and he saw a dump truck moving towards him. It was a 500-h.p. job – twice the height of a man with a cable drum in front protected by steel bars in an outward-turned V, like a battering-ram. Its pistons hammered like batteries of machine-guns. A Titanotherium!

Hood swung up his shovel, extended the neck and made a downward snatch-bite at the oncoming monster. The teeth hit the protecting steel hood over the cab. ripped a section away. The truck slithered but came on. Hood lifted the shovel head – seeing the enemy shovel dipping in – and struck again. The teeth tore into the bonnet and ripped away the radiator in a spout of water. As the truck stopped, there was the rattle of earth and rock on Hood's roof. The enemy shovel was dumping its load on him.

The armoured window above his head held. Involuntarily, Hood ducked, expected the enemy bucket to follow with a downward crunch through the cabin roof. In desperation, he threw the left-hand side lever, felt the gear engage and his whole machine moved slowly on its creepers. The enemy swung into his stern and jolted him to a halt.

He flung his bucket up, teeth rampant, and aimed for the cabin. He could see the driver through the front window, working the levers. He could scoop him out like a whelk!

A crash behind him shook his cabin and he ducked in the seat, seeing a massive steel hook withdrawing behind him through the cabin roof. Hood gasped. They had started another machine against him.

He threw in the crawlers, at the same time pivoting the cabinet. He saw it. Its 80-foot boom soared above him – a wrist-action drag-shovel, far bigger than his own, but instead of a bucket, a heavy-duty rock ripper like a beak of a gigantic hooked tin-opener. The hook was poised.

Hood swung at it. But his bucket seemed merely to paw the new machine. He could not discover how to accelerate the creeper speed. With another terrifying crash the ripper claw came down on the housing alongside him. Three feet nearer and he would have been pulped!

Hood pivoted. His damaged machine was making a loud grinding noise. He saw the snout of the other shovel swinging at his base, obviously with the idea of lifting and tipping him over. His machine tilted. He looked out and saw his crawlers on the edge of a sharp drop. He swung the boom arm, wrenched at the door as the machine lurched again. At the same moment, the cabin seemed to disintegrate, he was thrown off his feet with a fierce blow on the head and in a tangle of deafening noise blacked out.

CHAPTER NINE

HE HEARD the gentle sound of a mountain near by. The smell of aromatic wood drifted over to him, mingling with the heavy scent of flowers. His body was reclining comfortably among cushions. The surroundings were full of sunshine. Gradually the blurred edges of consciousness came together, things focused.

Hood looked round. Through an archway he saw the colonnade, a statue, the long still pool. He knew where he was.

He felt a curious inertia, a slightly absent effect, as if he were coming round from a drug, but otherwise he was at ease and felt no pain. He was propped up on the broad divan where he had been so expertly massaged by the girls when he had first entered the house. But they did not seem to be here now. He stirred, moved an arm. It wasn't tied up. He lifted the other; that was free too.

He heard a chuckle and looked round. Zagora was standing watching him. He was wearing a dark brown silk robe which came just below his knees and hung open showing his chest. He was smiling in frank enjoyment. He might have been watching a favourite child at play.

'What were you expecting, Mr Hood – chains? Forgive me, I have not said good morning. I trust you are comfortable? The small restriction on your movement is not troublesome? Every situation, of course, has its convention. Life demands the observance of a minimum of rules and so I am obliged to conform – I who normally shrink from convention, Mr Hood, I assure you, as much as you do yourself. You will find you cannot move your legs. We have, as they say, "taken care" of them. The method is perhaps not textbook.'

Hood was trying to move from the sitting position but couldn't work his leg muscles. The lower half of his body was insensible. He guessed they had given him an injection.

'I do not know what method your so splendid specialists Mr Sykes and Mr Fairbairn would recommend in the circumstances. What do you say, Mr Hood?'

Sykes and Fairbairn were the two ex-Shanghai policemen whose methods in unarmed combat had been taught to a selected number of Secret Service men.

Among other things, Hood had been through an especially tough course on how to fight in a room, using the furniture.

Hood was trying to clear his thoughts, to get his mind moving. They had taken his jacket again – it seemed compulsive with Zagora – but otherwise had left him his clothes and cleaned his shoes of mud.

'You are not in too much pain, Mr Hood?' Zagora chuckled again. 'The woman had bad teeth, as you discovered. But you did not treat her well.'

The recollection of the fight in the excavation came back to Hood's mind. What had happened to Tiara? Zagora was watching him closely. 'You need not feel any alarm about Lady Evenly,' he said. 'She was muddy when we found her but otherwise unharmed. She enjoyed a bath – I may say I attended her in it myself.'

Hood clamped his lips shut. Emotions now were pointless and he knew he must harbour his strength.

Zagora took a turn to the fountain and came back. 'It will be no surprise to you, Mr Hood, to hear that I have arranged for you to die.' He gave a deprecatory shrug. 'Again, we are both victims of convention, are we not? I do not really see what else I can do. I may say that in our arrangements we do not usually go to such trouble. But I felt that you had been to some trouble over *us* and I had in fairness – what the French call le fairplay, n'est-ce pas? – to keep up. There are moral standards. One has one's obligations. The trouble with the world, don't you find, Mr Hood, is the deplorable erosion of duty?'

Hood was running his hand over his legs. His dread was that the numbness might be concealing torn muscles, a broken bone; but it was hard to tell. He hated Zagora's guts and he wanted to go on hating them – because he knew that when he stopped he wouldn't want to live any more.

Zagora strode across the room and back. He looked formidable in his power and confidence.

'You are acquainted, of course, with the Parsees' method of disposing of their dead, Mr Hood? I have always thought it simple, hygienic, excellent in every way – above all economical. The Parsees are admirably practical people and I follow humbly in their footsteps.'

Hood had a mental picture of the Towers of Silence in Bombay, as he had often seen them – the mass of foliage hiding the surrounding wall, the iron gates, the vultures planing overhead on their great wings or lumbering up from the bodies offered within. They picked the bones clean in no time. In the Indian heat, the system of feeding the dead to vultures was sanity itself. And what of the body, once life had gone? Yet Hood had never looked up at the obscene bunches perched in the tops of the trees without an inner shudder. Illogical as it was, he knew he would hate to deliver over to those evil beaks even the lifeless remnant of someone he had once loved.

Zagora shot him a look. 'The Indian vultures naturally eat only the dead. Vultures are cautious creatures. But Balek – you have seen Balek? Yes, of course – Balek has improved on this. He has trained the vulture we have here to eat food that moves.' He gave a laugh.

'You are a naturalist, Mr Hood? No? That is a pity. You would realize what an achievement that is. It is stupendous. It means the deflection of an immensely strong congenital trait; it is only conceivable with someone who has such an affinity to birds as Balek. His vulture will tackle living things.'

Zagora paused briefly. 'You will be able to observe all this yourself, Mr Hood. You will have, what do you call it, a grandstand seat? It is a slowish business; and, of course, if the bird is not over-hungry, it will eat a portion of you – some tender morsel here or there, a snack – and return for further meals later. You will have time for contemplation, Mr Hood, between meal-times. You will become a determined ruminant!'

Hood said grimly: 'I shall be ruminating on your damnation, Zagora.' Lightly kneading his thigh muscle, he had the impression that the numbness was wearing off.

Zagora showed his teeth. 'Excellent! I am bound to say

I admire you, Mr Hood. You have the splendid English gift of not facing the unpleasant fact. But I am anxious that our hospitality should be worthy of this occasion. It is not every day we are privileged to remove one of Her Majesty's perfect gentle knights.

'Is there something you would care for, Mr Hood? What would give you most enjoyment for these last fifteen minutes? You are a man of imagination. And, after all, it is a great English tradition – the condemned man, the special last breakfast, is it not? There are natural limits – again we are both prisoners of convention – but if there is something refreshing, amusing, titillating, I can offer, please say the word.' He clapped his hands. Efim came in.

Hood said: 'I'd like a martini and a cigarette.' He strove with all his mental force to think of how to gain time. His thoughts were empty. But the paralysing drug in his legs was definitely dissipating.

Zagora gave the order and Efim went out.

'Who's your master for this operation, Zagora?' Hood said.

'Master!' Zagora flung round with a whirl of his robe. But he quickly controlled himself and laughed. 'That is a splendid convention too, Mr Hood, is it not? By the rules, I should now explain to you, in detail, all my most interesting past iniquities. I should tell you, further, my deepest motives and the little touches of technique that give colour and verve' – he laughed again – 'I should provide you with all the evidence you need to convince you of my villainy and how I propose pursuing evil in the future.' He gave Hood a penetrating look. 'You are being puerile. You are damning my respect for you, Mr Hood.'

He strode to the far side of the room, called out through one of the arched window openings and waited there a moment until Balek appeared. Zagora stood articulating sounds which Hood could make nothing of. Then Balek moved away and Zagora returned as Efim came in. Efim carried a tray with one glass of drink. He paused, glancing at Zagora. Hood was measuring distances, easing himself towards the foot of the divan.

Zagora nodded. Efim advanced towards Hood. The small elegant crystal glass had a beautiful design engraved on it. Hood put one fist on the divan behind his back, extended the other hand and took the martini. He drank some. 'And my last cigarette?' he said.

Efim nodded and turned away. Hood smashed the top of the glass on his kneecap, gave a mighty downward thrust with his spare arm on the divan. He was on his feet, reaching out to jab the broken glass into Zagora's eyes. His legs seemed dead weights ... the distance was too great ... he was falling.

Zagora stepped back. Then as Hood tottered, trying madly to hitch himself forward, a blow crashed on his head and he passed out.

The first thing he noticed was the stench. The open sky was above. The sun was still high. There were a few clouds, He was bound, lying painfully and awkwardly on his back. His arms were underneath him. He could move his fingers, his feet a little and his head. He rolled on to one side and felt the binding. It was wire. Tearing pain from the movement ran up his legs and left him gasping. But it meant that the effect of the drug had passed.

The stench was putrescent and he realized that it came from his own body. He was stripped to the waist. He looked down and saw that he was smeared with a greyish paste like dripping. It was this that stank. Hood understood. They had trussed him up and plastered him with it so that he would smell like carrion for the vulture's benefit.

Apart from the terrible pain in his legs, Hood felt vaguely muzzy. There was a bulbous stone balustrade beyond which he could see part of a tree. It seemed to be somewhere in the grounds of Kuan-t'eng. He saw that he was lying on a flat roof. Beyond his feet was a door, shut. The surrounding roof was littered with droppings and bits of decayed meat and refuse. He craned his head and looked behind him. The vulture was perched on the balustrade watching him.

A shutter of wrinkled skin flicked down over the eye. Hood was horrified at the bird's size. The bald crooked neck hung out of the shoulders as if the bird were hunching itself malevolently. Without warning it hopped down heavily with a scratching of its claws. It walked towards Hood.

Hood shouted at it. The vulture stopped, stood there facing him. It was two feet away. It came a short step nearer. It was approaching his head. Hood thought it would go first for his eyes, then perhaps for the wound in his neck. He told himself he must try to keep moving; there was a small chance that it would discourage the creature.

The vulture edged closer. With horror Hood saw the neck extend in readiness to strike. He spat at it. The vulture drew back, turned and walked two steps level with his chest. Before Hood could try to counter it, the hooked beak darted out and caught his chest just below the nipple. Hood yelled. The beak had opened the skin in the fleshiest part of the chest – an expert attack.

He felt the trickle of blood. The bird walked in and gave another quick slash – and Hood had a momentary vision of the thing perched on his ribcage, burying its head in his guts, rooting around and tearing bits out. He hoped he would be dead before the process went too far. The cold eye watched him.

The neck jerked, the vulture caught a strip of flesh at the edge of the wound and tugged on it. Hood shouted with pain and the bird ran away several paces, somewhat alarmed. It sprang up on to the balustrade just over him. For a moment it did not move, then jumped down, landing on his belly with its head dipping over his crutch. Violently Hood rolled himself and yelled. The vulture blustered off and retired to a distance. It walked about, taking no notice of him, pecked at a strip of dried gristle among the scattered scraps from earlier meals. It evidently had an appetite.

Hood felt exhausted and nauseated. He shook his head. Must stay awake. As soon as the vulture saw he was not moving it would be at his eyes.

He strained at the wire; but it was an expert tie. Two ends had been twisted into a joint close to his hand. He tried to untwist them but could only manage to separate the two ends.

He lifted his head. The vulture was temporarily ignoring him. Hood noticed electric wiring running along the bottom of the parapet, evidently a light lead. There was a single plug just beyond his feet. Evidently the roof had at some time been used as a terrace and the light brought up in consequence.

He rolled over, his back to the vulture and with an up and down traction movement of his feet began to inch towards the plug. The vulture walked over to him again. Hood hissed and shouted, making it halt again. He was level with the light plug. He brought his hands into position, then rolled over so that his fingers touched it. This left him facing the vulture. The beak was three feet from his eyes.

Hood gritted his teeth. His fingers behind him found the plug. The vulture stood motionless. Hood managed to press the ends of wire farther apart. He sent up a prayer that there was current in the plug. He pushed one end of the wire in and waited.

The vulture came right up to him. He forced himself to lie still while the creature dug at his chest. He said: 'Jesus!' under his breath. He wanted to yell. The vulture bent over him, touching him – he jabbed the other end of the wire in and jolted at the shock and flash as the current passed into the wire round him and shorted.

There was a wild flutter of feathers; the bird seemed to be thrown off its feet with fright or shock. Then it was on the far side of the terrace twitching oddly. That's fixed you for a bit, you bastard. Hood thought.

But it had been a one-time shot. There would be no more help from that plug. He forced his knees up with all his strength, grimacing with pain as the wire cut into him. But when he relaxed, the wire had loosened.

He ignored the vulture, rolled over and hoisted his bound ankles on to the stone base of the balustrade, and began working his knees up and down, sawing the wire along the stone edge. It rasped his skin and he was soon sawing in blood. He tightened his lips and weighed down hard on the wire to give the action more effect. It was interminable. He had to keep stopping.

At last the wire gave. He worked his feet, loosening the binding. Only one coil came away. He had to go back to the rough stone edge again. The wire would not break!

The vulture seemed to be recovering. It was blinking at him menacingly. It took a step forward. Hood sawed wildly with his legs; a coil snapped. He strained his ankles apart. He rolled again, pushing his knees against the parapet. The saw action was easier now but there were multiple coils of the wire to sever.

Hood was sweating. The wound on his chest where the vulture had bitten into him was stinging with pain. But now his hope was quintupled.

The vulture seemed to sense that Hood was eluding it. It spread its wings as if it wanted to be sure of a quick take-off and blustered over to him. The beak came for his eyes. Hood twisted his head right and left. He butted the bird's head and the vulture stepped back once more.

Strands of wire round Hood's knees snapped. He used all his strength to force his knees apart, jack-knifed them up and staggered unsteadily to his feet. The vulture jumped into the air and Hood fell over backwards as it hit him. He got up, butting it.

Now Hood knew he could sever the wire round his arms if he could keep at it long enough. But the frustrated vulture was attacking and left him no chance. It knocked him over again. He told himself that this was the crunch. He must make one mighty effort or it would kill him. One well-aimed slash at his jugular...

He rolled to the balustrade and began rasping the wire at his wrists against the stone. Again, the stone edge stripped his skin. The vulture swooped. Hood threw up his foot and landed a solid kick as the bird descended. It went sideways, a black mass of feathers, and landed awkwardly four feet away. It stood looking at Hood with its shoulders hunched. It looked as if it were cursing him. Hood's mouth sagged. He was working furiously at the wire.

The vulture leapt up on to the balustrade just above him. Hood flipped over on his back and lashed out with both feet. The vulture was airborne before he got there, did a fast turn behind Hood's head and jerked out its open beak. The wicked hook gashed Hood's scalp slipped and closed on his ear. Hood yelled, butted backwards with his head, wincing at the tearing of his ear. The bird let go and retreated again.

The wire was still holding. Hood flopped exhausted. When he moved a moment later, one wrist seemed freer. He forced the thumb inwards into the palm, extended his fingers to make the hand as narrow as he could, and pulled. The hand slid halfway out of the wire coils and the next minute Hood had it free.

He got to his feet. The vulture flew at him. Hood ducked his head and jabbed with his elbow. The bird's claws ripped along his arm. He was struggling to liberate his other arm which was still attached and entangled in wire. The vulture soared and wheeled in from above, claws extended.

Hood had a terror of the thing fastening itself on his back. Perhaps it was the exhaustion of the fight, the release of tension; he wrenched his arm free. He was crouching, ducking away, irrational fear in his soul. The talons sank into his shoulder and he flung round, striking out wildly and yelling. He tripped in a tangled length of wire, snatched it up and jumped forward. The vulture was evidently surprised by the rapid transition to attack. Catching it momentarily off balance, Hood landed a heavy kick which knocked it over and stunned it.

Hood was reeling. He threw a loop of the wire over its head and jerked with all his force. The bird came over backwards, wings out; but before it could recover, Hood jumped on its head with joined feet and stamped. He winced as the bone crunched. The bird made him sick. He staggered over to the far balustrade. The vulture was making scratching sounds in its agony. He wanted to vomit. He hung over the balustrade. He sagged to his knees, clinging to the balustrade, head drooping. Then he hauled himself upright, shook his head. He got to his feet, gave himself a few minutes. He had a raging thirst. He noticed they had taken away his belt. Then he walked over to the door and pulled it open. There was a short flight of stone steps down.

Hood went down.

The place was a small disused pavilion, evidently given over to the vulture, with bare filthy rooms – all the window-panes knocked out – littered with scraps and droppings. Outside, a tap stuck out from the wall. He put his head under it and drank gratefully from the falling column of water.

Hood stood in the cover of the trees looking round. He could see the main house in the distance across the grounds. Behind him was the mountain. There seemed to be nobody about. It was early afternoon.

Keeping to the cover of the trees and shrubs, he worked his way round to the fence and found the place where he had climbed over. The rope had gone and they had broken off the bracket. That was that! He followed the fence down, watching the house through the cover. It was shuttered. He kept checking from different angles but couldn't see any activity. He left the shrubbery and ran across the grass. Everything was locked. They had cleared out in a hurry.

He went round the house. One of the shutters, he noticed, was fastened by a padlock. There was a U-type bicycle padlock on the next window-sill; but the shutter there was locked from the inside.

There was no point in trying to force an entrance. He ached for a cigarette, a chance to remove the stinking grease – his thoughts did not move beyond that. He seemed to remember the garage block was on the far side of the house, turned towards it and Balek came round the corner, six feet away.

Hood's heart jolted. He took in the thin body and arms, the head with the great osteosis beak. The creature's reach with those arms must be phenomenal. Hood felt dead beat after the fight with the vulture. And he knew that what was coming was not going to be agreeable. His eyes shifted quickly in search of some weapon; he snatched the bicycle lock from the window-sill, twisted the U-hook out and crouched. Balek pitched forward.

Balek did a rapid feinting move with his arms that momentarily surprised Hood and before Hood could react, had weaved in, swung his head under Hood's guard. The beak caught Hood's chest with a fearful smash. Hood went backwards. But Balek's grasp slipped on the grease and Hood fell free.

He scrabbled up. Balek moved at tremendous speed, circled him and Hood was still turning as Balek came in again, pinning his arms to his sides and smashed the beak against his chest – and again.

Hood broke the grip. There was confused grappling. Hood thanked God for the grease – it was saving him now! Balek couldn't keep hold. As the beak hit his chest again, Hood's left grasped Balek's hair, he pulled the head back and jabbed the U-hook into Balek's face. It hit the bony structure and slipped upwards into the eye.

Balek gave an ear-piercing screech. Hood knew he ought to jag down hard, but couldn't. Balek's hand was clawing at his face. The wound seemed to ruin his coordination all at once. Hood heaved him off and threw an armlock round his neck. Balek was making a cawing sound in his throat. Hood clamped his jaw, heaved and broke the neck. The long thin body sagged. Hood dropped it.

He stood gasping. He was still holding the U-lock and let it drop in disgust. He walked queasily away. He felt a clammy sweat on his forehead and the backs of his hands. He stood leaning against the wall. Presently he felt better. He went round the house and crossed to the garage block, smashed a small window and climbed in.

The Mercedes was there. He helped himself to tools from the work-bench, forced the main door and rolled it up. He scraped the worst of the grease off, cleaned up further with petrol and cotton waste and put on an overall coat that he found hanging up. As usual the shoulders cracked and the sleeves came halfway up his forearms; but it would have to do.

He climbed into the Mercedes and suddenly flopped. He thought he was going to faint. He had to lie there keeled over, his face ashen, a tremor on his hands, until gradually it passed. Presently he was able to sit up. He moistened his lips, gripped the steering wheel and pulled the car out.

The gatehouse was empty. He went in and opened the gate and drove the car out. On second thoughts, he shut the gate behind him; police inquiries wouldn't help.

He slammed the car door and swung down the road toward Belluno.

CHAPTER TEN

A MOTORBOAT hooted on the Grand Canal. Hood lay soaking in the bath. It seemed to him that he could never bathe enough to get the stench of that grease off him; and it seemed that he could never rid his mind of the fights with Balek and the woman gatekeeper. It was late morning and he felt ragged. But they had accomplished a good deal since he had reached Venice the evening before.

To begin with he had sent a long signal to Conder outlining the situation. He had consulted with Arthur Graff. They had decided to send one of Graff's confidential men up to Belluno to see what he could learn and Graff had been busy tipping off his various contacts to report if they saw or heard of Tiara or the other women Hood had seen who could hardly all have dispersed without trace.

Graff, it was plain, was miserably uncomfortable. Hood felt sure Zagora was still in the area and would reappear. In any event, they couldn't move in any direction until they had some clue.

Hood had then had Giulio's personal doctor go over his injuries; his neck needed three stitches and the vulture had cut his scalp quite severely; but the rest were not too bad. He had bought another gun. After this, Graff had arranged for him to see Dr Martino, a local physician who had worked in the East and was up in tropical medicine.

Dr Martino was a good-looking, fair-haired Piedmontese of about thirty-eight, a cultured man. His consulting-room had a Tiepolo on the ceiling.

'Laughing death?' Martino said, when Hood had explained that this was what he was interested in. 'You mean *kuru*? It's a very mysterious thing. It was only described for the first time about ten years ago, you know. It occurs in New Guinea, up in the eastern hills. Rough country. One of the oddest things about it is that it has been largely confined to the Fore tribe. There are only about 35,000 of them and they live in an area of about 1,000 square miles. Some members of the tribes the Fore marry into also get it. But apart from these, it is now beginning to spread outside.

'It is primarily a disease of women and children – though not exclusively – and affects what we call motor co-ordination. It's quite characteristic. The women who get it start walking in a curiously clumsy way – their motor activity isn't co-ordinating properly. Then they get shivering, trembling spells – the word *kuru* means trembling – and if they are excited, the shiver becomes worse. When this shivering or trembling gets chronic, the least excitement sets off wild laughter. It has been described as "inordinate laughter" and of course that is where the name comes from. The victim usually dies inside a year.'

'Is it always fatal, then?' Hood asked.

'It is very deadly. Fewer than ten per cent of victims recover. The odd thing is that a lot of these who are regarded as hopeless cases recover overnight – in a few hours. This, we believe, is because they have simply been compulsively mimicking the real *kuru* syndrome. Mimetism, you know, is an enormously potent force in human affairs, far more than people realize – you know how "catching" laughter can be ordinarily – and it so happens that this sick laughter compels some people to mimic it or, if you like, to "catch" it, even more than ordinary laughter does. But these people haven't really got the disease and so are "cured" overnight.'

'What's the cause?'

'That's altogether a mystery. It is degeneration of the central nervous system. It seems that to get it or rather to *spread* it, you have to have lived in the *kuru* region of New Guinea and to possess the *kuru* gene. But you probably also have to come into contact with a virus or some other infective agent.'

'In other words,' Hood said, 'because you possess the gene, the virus acts on you and you develop the disease or pass it on?'

'Something like that.'

Hood thought for a moment. 'I suppose a woman with *kuru* would become very dependent on other people?'

'Oh, of course, increasingly dependent. It has been used by some of the headmen in New Guinea to reduce enemies and others to complete dependence on them. How they do it nobody knows. It reduces will-power to nothing, of course.'

'So they seem to be able to transmit it at will?'

'That's very difficult to say; but it looks like it.'

'And in the end, the victim laughs herself to death?'

'That's it.'

That had been enough. Hood had walked back to the hotel thinking of the woman who had come out laughing among the group at Zagora's, of the way Zagora had calmed her and her obvious dependence on him. Balek had transmitted the disease to her – just as he had to Diana Undermere – to bring her to absolute dependence on Zagora. Then that one unaccountable outburst of laughter from Tiara as they had run into the excavation came back to him. Had she been infected? Hood was completely shaken. He had paced the room in despairing restlessness, then fell into bed and slept like a log from sheer exhaustion.

Now, as he lay in the bath, he was waiting for Graff to report on what he had been able to find out about Zagora's movements.

Hood got out, dried himself and fixed his plaster dressings. The waiter wheeled in the breakfast trolley and Hood was just finishing when the phone rang to say that Signor Graff was below. A moment later, Arthur came in.

'Can I ring for something for you, Arthur?'

'No, thank you,' Graff said. 'I haven't much news yet. As far as I can make out they moved down here to Venice. It is difficult to discover whether they are still here. I would swear they have not used the airport, at all events, and my men at the railway station have not seen them.'

'Any news from Belluno?'

'Nothing.'

Hood lit a cigarette. Every hour they lost, he felt, made things more risky. Graff said: 'I am now going to try to see my special friend. That means I shall be out of touch for a few hours. I will ring you this afternoon.' The 'special friend', Hood understood, was the woman who had given Graff the earlier tip-off about Zagora. It was typically Venetian, the necessity for intermediaries, Hood recognized, and he could not curtail the process.

'Very well, Arthur.'

But when Graff had gone, Hood felt more restless and uneasy than before. The prospect of a block of several hours at this point got on his nerves. He felt he could not stay indoors. He stood at the window looking out on to the canal. Two big motor-barges were passing, loaded with coal and cement. A young baker in a white cap and apron with a basket on his back was ferrying across in a gondola, laughing and joking with the gondolier.

Hood went down and told the porter he would telephone in an hour for any messages, then walked out. A water-taxi was hitched at the landing stage and Hood took it round the heel of the canal to the Prefetura and walked through the back streets.

The small canals were green, still and soothing. He looked at the crumbling walls and the marvellous and changing succession of porches, stone figures and heads and arches. Men in barges were unloading cauliflowers and cases of beer outside Byzantine water-gates and others hauled Goya-esque sides of beef on hand trolleys up the steps of the bridges. He looked down the narrow grey impasse of the Ramo degli Armeni at the medieval buildings with heavily barred windows and the dark deep arches at each end. Washing hung with green plants above.

He walked on. The Piazza blazed with sun. There weren't many tourists but they all seemed to be Scandinavian with small white sailor caps. Sometimes they were all French or Japanese. It depended on the boatloads or plane arrivals.

He turned through the Piazetta to the lagoon. A fat sad blue-haired woman, American or English, was being rowed out on a gondola with all her trunks and luggage piled up behind her. She sat, in her hat, with folded hands while the gondolier shoved slowly against the current and she looked so melancholy. Farewell Venice, she was saying. She was leaving it behind. She looked as if she had decided to go away in a gondola because she knew she was never coming back. It moved Hood to watch her.

And of course there were such melancholy tones about Venice. He thought of the music in the Piazza San Marco at night when the orchestra played outside Quadri's – nothing so marvellously evocative as that. He heard it now, in the bright sunshine as he looked out over the water, faintly and unmistakably in his mind, the orchestras playing one after the other to the rows of chairs and customers. The weeping violins soared with the operatic selections and the musical comedy hits and the fruity solos, so sentimental and corny, the intertwining mingling of the strings echoing and hammering, fading and lifting in the great square, lost and sad echoes of palm lounges, other days, the past, the past, lifting up on those twining thirds, the music of cardboard kingdoms and loving hearts finding a way. The rows of black gondolas rocking at the Molo before him, now, were intermingled with the sweeping lifts of the violins and his shadow was stretching out on the grey stones and the water on which was superimposed, in his mind's eye, the great Piazza and the arches, the rows of chairs and the violinists' lighted music-stands.

He turned. The old sweet-seller in his white coat and blue trousers with his cellophane box of skewered toffees was still on his pitch outside the Doge's Palace. The lottery-ticket man was calling out: 'Loter – ia Capodanno Nation – ale. Centa cinquante mill – ione.' What the hell could centa cinquante millione mean to him?

Hood walked on over the bridges along the Riva dei Schiavoni. A big black-hulled liner with red and black funnel and green band – the superstructure as high as the Doge's Palace – was coming down the buoyed channel. As she reached the line of hotels, a tug swung out arrogantly from the quayside towards her, in no hurry, showing its confidence, and there was a shouted exchange between the two captains over the loud hailers. The tug was the *Maximus*. Hood liked the Venice tugs. They all had fine *us* names. He looked at the others tied up on the quayside; the *Strenuus*, the *Austerus*, the *Notus*, the *Titanus*.

The sad district of the public gardens and the sports ground stretched ahead. It was the other side of Venice, a scabrous slum. He went through the dusty gardens. A few elderly people were sitting on the benches, a child or two played. Under the arch he went into the Terra S.

Isepo and the Paludo Antonio – grim poverty. Rows of low slum tenements faced each other across the street. There was a separate family – if not two – to each room. Washing was slung out from side to side overhead. Small girls with ear-rings were skipping on the stone flags. Cats were mangy and they cringed too. No passer-by could fail to be seen here; everybody out of doors was under observation from twenty windows and doors at once. The smell of washing mingled with the smell of close-packed humanity.

He turned the corner, crossed a bridge and walked alongside a canal. The water was still and filthy. The once-noble houses were now all rotting tenements. Washing on pulleyed lines was slung across the canal. Radios screeched tinnily from the doorways, women shouted across to each other.

Hood turned back past the moss-covered statue to Garibaldi with its lion – the best lion in Venice – encrusted in moss with the water gently dripping and Garibaldi romantic and grandiloquent on top. Farther on, under a statue of Christ, there was the Cinema Garibaldi with a lurid poster.

He went into a café-gelateria and rang the hotel. There had been no message. It was a good clean café with a view of the lagoon. He sat drinking a campari-soda and smoking. The time was hanging heavily. He was still restless and when he had paid for the drink he walked back to the Schiavoni with the idea of going to the Academia and looking at the pictures to break his uneasiness. But he knew the clash of moods would be too sharp. He was in no state of mind to look at Veroneses or Bellinis or Tintorettos.

The *vaporetti* were taking on passengers all along the quay. He turned and boarded one, not caring greatly where it went since he could quickly return if it went too far afield. It was the Lido boat. He took his ticket and stood gazing back at the theatrical backdrop of the quay-side as it receded.

The boat landed him at the Santa Maria Elisabetta

landing stage. A middle-aged woman in black with dark glasses and a long pale face got off too. He thought he had seen her with the lottery-ticket seller near the Piazetta.

He crossed the road and headed down the broad straight avenue towards the beach. There was the indelible air of all the boarding-house holidays in the world, the cheap, knocked-up ineradicable imprint left behind by months of dusty and exhausted families, screaming children, one-day trippers and hard professional tourist-trimmers on the make. It was vulgar and, Hood had always thought, the ugliest thing in Venice. Festoons of light-bulbs hung from the plane trees over the café terraces. There was hardly anybody about. The café signs said 'Gelati' and 'Juke-box'. They had posters showing a dozen architectural gelati with descriptions in three languages.

Hood stopped at a rack of postcards. The woman in black was along the pavement behind him. She seemed to him strangely disturbing. But the next minute a small bald man came out of a café and stood speaking to her and Hood put the unpleasant impression down to his mood.

He went on down the road. At the far end he came to the flyblown public square with gravel, a few poplars and red wooden benches. To right and left, as far as he could see, the road ran, parallel with the sea, dead straight and empty. There wasn't a soul in sight. Even the two stalls piled with beach hats and scarves with Venice stencilled on them were deserted. A hoarding said 'Bar Dancing Ristorante Blue Moon'. Round the gardens, the wastepaper bins were stuffed full. They looked as if they'd still be full next year.

Romantic spot, Hood thought. Yet the atmosphere was thick enough to cut and in its way, the place responded to his frame of mind. He crossed the broad empty road. Before him the Adriatic lapped mildly in like soup. There was a rubbery purr and a trolley-bus went by behind. Hood glanced back and noticed the woman in black sitting alone on one of the red seats.

He turned away down the steps to the beach level. Below was a café with blue chairs outside and shops selling the terrible local glass and souvenirs. An engraved tile said 'I was in Venice and I thought of you'. The beach stretched empty on either side. Double and triple rows of bathing-huts, two feet apart, faced the sea, all shut off by a wooden fence. This was the cheap end of the Lido. The smart section was out of sight at the distant end of the road at the Excelsior Hotel and thereabouts.

He climbed back up the steps. Everything was quiet and peaceful. The woman in black was sitting on a nearer seat. She had black lace-up boots and a black lacepiece round her throat. Hood thought she looked like murder and he didn't like it.

Hood turned down the long road. It was warm and quiet. The saplings lining the road did not offer any shade. There was a fence between the road and the beach bathing-huts. He was walking on, passing nobody. The high white Edwardian façade of the Hotel des Bains, a place like a cliff, was shuttered. The clock at the top had stopped. It looked as if it had stopped to mark the death of Edward the Peacemaker and not got started again. A roadside hoarding for suntan cream said 'Stupenda abbronzatura ... naturale. Wundervoll braun ohne Sonnenbrand'. How d'ya like 'em? Stupenda abbronzatura or wundervoll braun?

He turned again. The woman was following. Hood felt vulnerable and a little sick. The woman filled him with unreasoning apprehension. It was mixed up with the emptiness of the long straight road, the quiet, the sun, with everything being deserted here.

There was the faint ambling clop-clop of a horse, the only sound. It was a solitary fiacre – going the other way.

He went on past the casino. Brown ribbed shutters were down over the windows. The enormous block of the Hotel Excelsior, domes, crenellations and chimneys like minarets, rose just ahead like an architect's nightmare.

Hood increased his pace. The main door was boarded up. The boards were worn, as if they had been nailed in place against a tribal raid years before. He looked in through the glass side door into the hall. It was deserted. Furniture was piled on the far side by the doors leading out to the terrace and the beach. Hood pushed the door. It was open. He went in.

He crossed the hall. On the far side he saw a group of workmen busy with rolls of carpet far down the corridor. The next minute he was out on the beach.

Fear – which somehow he could not cope with now – pressed him. He turned down the alley between the close rows of striped wooden bathing-huts, hurrying in the sand. There was nobody, not a sound. The bathing-huts seemed to multiply without end and in a flash he had the impression of walking into a mirror-like infinity of receding lines of striped bathing-huts.

He tried door after door. They were all locked. He ducked into a cross-alley to the next row. It was empty. But the bathing-huts were all locked here too. The stripes seemed to be twitching like a fantastic mobile or an optician's dazzle trick. He heard a faint sound and squeezed between two huts. A shadow silently flipped past. He turned back, crossed to the next row, immediately retreated – the black form was returning!

Hood ran hard between the identical rows of identical huts and pulled up. He stood close to a hut at the cross-alley, unable to decide to cross to the next row since he could not tell which way the woman was facing now. There was the sound of hard breathing. He pressed back against the wall of the hut, the woman went by three feet away, eyes staring ahead. She had taken off the blue glasses. The long pale face was beaded with sweat. She moved very energetically.

Hood waited until she had gone by, then stepped quickly across the alley and reached the bushes by the road. He scanned the road. Nobody in sight. He negotiated the fence, crossed over and walked rapidly into the side-street opposite. He stood behind a cigarette slot machine. The Lido was enveloped in its quiet deserted off-season afternoon sun.

In a moment, the woman appeared through the bushes. She looked up and down the road, then awkwardly climbed the fence. She turned away towards the Gran Viale Santa Maria Elisabetta, walking quickly.

Now Hood was the follower. He tailed her to the landing stage. Just before she took her ticket, a huge man with a pill head – Hood couldn't help thinking of a Henry Moore figure – came up to her and they stood speaking. The *vaporetto* arrived and they both got on. Hood remained under cover until it was well out, then he went to the water-taxi station and took one. Hood saw them get off at the Ponte del Vin, obviously because it was a Number 3 *vaporetto* and would take them too far round by the railway station. He made the water-taxi hang back.

Fortunately, Henry Moore was easy to spot and Hood saw the two board a Number 4 which headed up the Grand Canal.

Hood sat masked by the boatman and they followed discreetly. The two got off at the Rialto Bridge and walked into the crowded street by the canal, then turned off down a small street towards San Canciano's. Hood had paid his man and followed. They turned again and stopped at a big house with a great church-like stone façade and steps up to a massive front door. They rang and while they waited on the steps, another man, a thin whippet-faced man with quick movements, came up. They exchanged a few words, the door opened and they all went in. Hood walked away. He noted the number 3712A Calle Maggio.

At the hotel there was a message from Graff. Hood stood in the hall reading it. 'I expect to see you later. Meantime, Miss Lake has sent me word that she will be at 1960B Calle Callino this evening and has news for you there. Best take precautions and go about dusk so as not to be seen. AG.'

Miss Lake? Momentarily he was checked, then got it; of course – Malaren. And she was his ally.

He went up to his room and rang Graff. Graff was not yet back but was expected. Hood cursed and waited impatiently for half an hour. He rang for the waiter and told him to bring a double Chivas Regal whisky with Perrier; he didn't need to say 'No ice' – they didn't serve whisky with ice at Giulio's.

Hood felt disturbed by the Lido episode. It had given him a chill. Or maybe it was premonition; he didn't know. He drank the whisky, waiting. When he rang Graff again and Arthur had still not returned, he gave up. He checked his new Spanish Starfire automatic. He didn't care for automatics but the Starfire had an external hammer and weighed only fourteen and a half ounces with a six-shot clip of ·38s. It was the best gun he had been able to get. The alternatives were a Beretta Cougar which was heavier and didn't carry a bigger punch or hefty German guns. He had taken the Spaniard.

He went downstairs and stood in the hall looking on the town-plan for the Calle Callino. It was a small street near the Ghetto Nuovo, in the northern part of the city. The shortest way was to take a motorboat up the Grand Canal. But Hood decided that was a thing to avoid; it was too public. If Zagora was on the look-out, he would be picked up before he had reached the Rialto Bridge.

He went through the back streets to the Ponte della Statione and turned briskly into the railway station. The Turin train was at platform 3. Hood walked to the head and climbed in. The train was not starting for another thirty-five minutes and was still empty.

He stood watching the platform, then walked slowly back down the corridor. A fat man approached from the far end of the second coach and Hood stepped back into a carriage just in time as he made to squeeze by. When the man had passed, Hood had a shudder thinking what the guy could have done with a knife. Christ! He was getting soft and careless – and jumpy. At the other end, he got down and walked away. He was pretty sure he wasn't being followed.

He turned along the Lista di Spagna and crossed the small bridge by St Jeremiah's church. For a moment, he had asked himself how Malaren should have known to send the message to Graff. She must have got it from Tiara. This, and the 'Miss Lake' authenticated it. Moreover, it indicated – though it didn't prove – that Zagora was in Venice.

The Rio Terra San Leonardo was crowded and bustling. Shops were beginning to light up. There were stalls displaying fruit, sausage, cheese. Egg-sellers were calling out 'Freschi!' This was another part of the city Hood liked to come to. He turned left up the narrow Calle de Rabbia which led to the ghetto on its octagonal island, like a fortress, still with its three gates which, in the past, had been locked at nightfall with Christian guards posted in boats on the surrounding canals.

Floating refuse littered the water. He looked up at the tall brick houses. Once the windows had been blocked up by decree, so that the ghetto turned blank walls to the city until the Marangona rang from the Piazza San Marco in the morning and the gates were reopened.

He crossed the wooden bridge under the arch into the ghetto square, the Campo del Ghetto Nuovo – peeling redbrick medieval tenements, six storeys high, still standing with their windows outlined in stone and iron braces like metal plasters. It was an area of fine character.

Hood stood watching the pedestrians who came across the bridge. Nobody he had spotted before. He went over the wide canal beyond and turned left. The Calle Callino was a small empty street with poor houses and one or two blind ruins. Number 1960B was at the far end.

It was a small decayed two-storey house with a stained façade, a broken balcony and arched windows with pilasters. Most of the windows were shuttered and dirty lace curtains hung at the others. Hood didn't much like it. But this, he supposed, when it came to it, was about what he could have expected.

He rang the bell at the street door. No answer. The door was locked. The small iron grille in the door was covered inside with paper. He looked through a hole in it into a dim passage. Then he saw a string hanging inside the grille, fished it out and found the door-key at the end. He went in.

Hood took out his gun and stood inside the door listening. He heard a faint sound from above; rats. He looked back into the street again. It was growing darker.

A room on the left of the entrance was locked. He went down the passage. At the end were two more dingy rooms, one with tall-backed broken chairs, a dusty mirror and a glass-fronted book-case; the other a barely furnished kitchen with linoleum on the floor. He looked round for some letter or note but couldn't see anything.

Hood's steps grated on the gritty tiles of the passage as he walked back towards the stairs. The place didn't look much lived in. He stood at the bottom of the stairs with his gun ready, looking up. The sound from above was repeated.

Very cautiously, he went up. The stairs were darker than the passage. At the top, he stopped on the landing, hardly breathing. His eyes were exploring. There were two ugly dark-painted doors with white porcelain knobs which stood out in the gloom. He covered the first, turned the knob, kicked it open. He stood covering it, then moved in. The room was empty.

He turned back on the landing for the other door and, as he crossed towards it, looked down the corridor leading towards the back. There was a dim glow of light at the end. Then his nerves jagged as he saw a figure moving in the end room and throwing shadows on the wall and ceiling.

He crouched, ready to shoot. The figure made a stifled sound as if it were trying to call out. It was somebody tied up in a heavy high-backed chair – a girl. Her face was puffed. He went forward. It was Malaren, with a gag in her mouth.

As he went towards her, she emitted a series of muffled

cries and struggled to free herself. She was widening her eyes at him.

Hood paused. It struck him that she had been scared by his appearance with the gun. He started to speak: 'It's all right, Malaren, it's me – not going to hurt you.' But he felt there was something else.

Abruptly she gave signs of distress, her head sagged. He saw she had fainted and jumped forward towards the door of the room. And at the last second he sensed – as some reflex worked – or he saw at that instant, the faint booby-trap line across his path, threw himself down, trying to twist away, to avoid it – and failed, fell on it and the muffled burst of three almost simultaneous shots reverberated through the empty house.

Hood lay flat, gun ready, listening. He felt his skin creeping as it did when he expected to be hit by a bullet. He got up. Malaren sagged in the chair. The room stank of powder. He saw that she had been shot in the middle of the body. But the booby-trap had been meant to get him too and only his last-minute action in flinging himself down had saved him.

He was inside the room, swinging his gun round at empty walls. There was a smoking oil lamp on the floor, nothing else. He turned swiftly to Malaren and lifted her chin, in agony at having done this to her. They had stuffed her mouth with cotton-wool. He pulled it out. She was unconscious.

He tore at the cords lashing her to the chair. She was in a green and white cotton dress. Oh God, Hood thought; I'm guilty. I'm responsible. I was guilty from the start with this kid. They did this to her because of me. I involved her.

He paused once to look round for the guns they had used; but he couldn't see how they were placed. It was a murderous tie-up with water-shrunken cord cutting into her arms and legs. He freed her in the end.

He took her in his arms and lifted her out of the chair and moved towards the door. But she had come round and whispered: 'No. Let me stay with you.' He stood there, uncertain what to do. She was obviously badly hurt and needed rapid care.

'Please ... sir.... Just hold me. Don't take me away now.'

'I must get you to a hospital,' he said.

'Please. That is no good now.'

'I'll stay with you.' He knelt gently with her and sat cradling her in his arms.

Softly she said: 'I tried to warn you.'

'I know....' Hood felt he was being torn apart. 'Will you forgive me, Malaren? I did it, I tripped that line and I wouldn't have hurt you for the world. You know that?'

'Yes.'

'You know I wouldn't hurt you, don't you, though?'

'You mustn't say these things. You didn't do me harm.'

He wanted to know about Zagora. But how could he ask her at such a moment; and who knew what secret belief in that evil man she still had? 'Malaren, let me take you to a hospital quickly. I'll stay with you, I swear I won't leave you a minute.'

Her voice was fainter. 'No. Only a few minutes. Hold me in your arms.'

'Dear Malaren.' Hood could not speak.

She said: 'Do you still think it's pretty for a girl to be called after a lake?'

'Yes, and you're the prettiest girl I know.'

She drew in her breath as if the pain were worse. He supported her. She said: 'Thank you for coming up to the mountain.'

'Thank you for everything you did.' (And loaded with guilt, he wanted to say: I wish I were coming in now again for the first time; I'd do things differently, Malaren, oh Christ, I would.)

'I'm glad you came,' she said.

'I am too. I'm glad.' It was all he could think of to say. 'I'm glad.'

'Would you kiss me, sir?'

He kissed her cheek, then gently her lips.

She was quiet. In a moment she said: 'Sir, please

hold—' She did not finish. There was no movement, just a gentle relaxation.

He saw she was dead.

Hood stayed there holding the dead girl. He didn't move. He was overcome. He did not know what to do. He stayed there. His mind refused to work and the feelings of the moment even kept away his hatred for Zagora.

He laid her down and stood up in the flickering light of the lamp. He knew he could not take her out of the house, dare not tell the police because of the complications it would involve to the ruin of his assignment. But it was like hitting her to walk out and leave her there. What could he do?

He stepped over and blew the lamp out and the smell of smoke curled up round him. The house was dark now. He wondered if they hadn't set up another trap for him – a tip-off to the police to call at the house, in case he had escaped. He said 'Goodbye, Malaren, and bless you', and felt his way along the passage, down the stairs and along to the front door.

He looked out. The street lamp opposite was alight. He could hear somebody talking a little way off and the sound of a radio. He let himself out, turned swiftly in the doorway, locked the door and slipped the key back inside through the grille.

Two women were standing to the left. He walked the other way, crossed the bridge opposite and turned along the canal, quickening his pace. He made his way back on foot across the Canal Della Misericordia and on impulse turned into the Santi Apostoli church and lit a candle. He crossed the Rialto Bridge and went through the Campo di Frari and did not stop until he reached the hotel.

He picked up the telephone and called Graff. His eyes were cold.

Graff, the housekeeper said, was still away. Hood hung up. He rang for the waiter and had him bring a double gin and French – Gordon's and Noilly Prat. Then he sat down and wrote out a careful signal to Conder, addressed to the Imperial Watch Company (the SIS cover office), bringing him up to date. Could Whitney and two other SIS men stand by, he asked? Hood was convinced that Zagora was not going to let things rest as they were. In the meantime, Chuck had his hands full watching Tickle in London.

He went downstairs and had Giulio send a man with the cable to the commercial cable office at the station which stayed open late. He ordered another gin and French and sat with it in the small inner salon which had a barred window looking out on to the side canal.

The salon was elegant, comfortable and empty. The soft-shaded lamps, one in dark red with a *passementerie* fringe, shed their light on the silk and satin chair coverings, on the black Chinese lacquer cabinet and its gilded console, on Giulio's Nymphenburg heads and the three eighteenth-century Chinese glazed figures. He could not relax and enjoy it. Malaren's death had cast a pall over everything. He nursed the cold anger in his mind.

At 8.30 he rang Arthur Graff again. The number rang for a long time, then the housekeeper answered. She had been on the stairs, on her way out, she said, and had come back to catch the call. Graff had rung during the afternoon to say he would be back late and would see Hood early in the morning. She had been coming round to tell him this on her way home.

This seemed to Hood a bit circuitous. But Graff was obviously being careful and not wanting to put the finger on him by ringing him direct from wherever he was.

Hood ate a lonely dinner. The past twenty-four hours, he felt, had been an ominous lull – before the lightning started. Zagora now knew that he had escaped the booby-trap; and that could only have unpleasant results. If Graff produced the goods, they would have to close in fast. In any event, Hood now had the house on the Calle Maggio to tackle – a line to the devil.

He was keyed up. He went to bed and turned out the light. He concentrated on the back of his eyelids and blocked off his thoughts with all the strength of his mind. It took him an hour to reach sleep.

CHAPTER ELEVEN

IT WAS a golden morning. He woke at seven o'clock, had breakfast on the roof terrace with the sun pouring warmly down on him. The water of the canal flashed. The golden nipple on the dome of San Stefano's glittered. Somebody in a passing gondola called out to someone else: 'Che bellissimo giorno!'

Sure, bellissimo, Hood thought. As the opening of a bad day, it was fine. Venice was too old for violence.

He went in and asked Paulo, the waiter, if they had had any luck with Signor Graff's number yet. They had been ringing, Paulo said, but had no reply. It was 8.25. Hood went down to his room, checked his gun, changed into a light pair of shoes and scribbled a note to Graff saying he'd gone to the Calle Maggio address and would be back. This he sealed and left downstairs.

He took a gondola ferry across the Grand Canal and walked through to the banking area behind the Piazza San Marco. Like all the cities in the world at this hour, Venice was busy with crowds going to work. He turned in through the bronze doors of the Credito Adriatico and asked for Signor Guardi. At this time of the morning? The under-manager smiled indulgently. Signor Guardi, the senior director, *might* come a little before noon. But in any event, his time was entirely occupied. If the Signor would care to write; matters could be dealt with by correspondence.

Hood was not impressed. His look conveyed no friendliness.

'Ring up Signor Guardi and tell him I am on the personal business of Count Walter de Rothsteil. Do it now.' Hood looked at him straight.

The under-manager's face changed. He said he had misunderstood. If the signor would be so good as to wait. The private office was at his disposal.

Twenty-four minutes later, Signor Guardi arrived with shaving-soap behind his ears. He had grey hair in romantic locks and a chiselled face. He looked like his own idea of a soldier-poet. He didn't like being hustled at this early hour, but he knew he couldn't do anything about it and the look of Hood confirmed this. Hood did not contribute to any illusion. He cut through some eloquent phrases about devoted service.

'You have a telex?'

'Yes, to our head office in Rome.'

'I have an urgent private communication to make to London. Kindly get through to your head office and have them call Rothsteil's in Rome. Rothsteil's have a direct telex line to London. The message is to be given to Count Walter de Rothsteil in the Lombard Street branch or to one of his brothers *personally*. I mean personally.'

The soldier-poet swallowed. Hood scared him.

'The message is this: I want to have a telex conversation with Lord Claymore at eleven o'clock GMT this morning and will he have Shakespeare with him. They will arrange for the telex link-up with his office here. Clear?'

Shakespeare was Conder's code name and the telex link with ICC would be arranged through The Circle's private telex exchange.

'Quite clear, Signor Hood.'

'The message is confidential. I wish you to keep the telex copy so that we can destroy it later.'

'Certainly, Signor.'

Hood looked straight at Guardi's eyes. 'You will deal with this personally, Signor Guardi.' It was not a question and there were no soft edges to Hood's voice. Guardi understood. 'Naturally, Signor Hood.'

Hood stood up. 'I'll be back at eleven o'clock.'

Outside, Hood turned through the streets behind the clock tower making for the Rialto. It was a Japanese day. There were Japanese tourists all over, smiling and taking photographs. At the Rialto, he walked north until he reached the Calle Maggio. He took it cautiously. The house presented its severe front. No activity. There was a café-gelateria at the corner from which he would be able to see the house at an angle. But he thought of look-outs – the three men last night.

Hood stood at the corner newspaper kiosk studying the magazines on display. The house looked formidably difficult to tackle. He couldn't see a way in.

He inspected the café again. An old man in a black longshoreman's cap was sitting at a table and there was a girl waitress. Hood bought *Il Gazzettino*, the excellent Venice paper, went in and ordered coffee. He sat drinking it, glancing at the paper and discreetly observing the house.

After five minutes, Henry Moore came out alone. Hood caught a glimpse of a thug male servant inside with the scar-tissue thick on his eyebrows. Then Moore walked on down the street. Hood thought of tailing him, then decided no. He watched him go. He was a big bastard. They had a lot of big bastards.

After that there was nothing for half an hour. It was ten-thirty-three. He paid and went out. He crossed the bridge and saw that the house gave on to a small green canal at the back. There was another bridge farther along, nearer the place. He went round reconnoitring. The usual water-gate gave directly on to the canal. Hood's jaw muscles were knotting and unknotting as he stood looking at it. It was going to be murder to take it that way.

He scanned the house next door. There was another water-gate and, above, an *altane*, a roof-terrace. But the big drop to the adjoining roof was professional acrobat stuff. He would have to come back.

He walked back to the bank. Guardi led him to the

telex room among the offices – an abrupt glimpse of a routine universe light-years distant from Zagora and all this episode. A young Italian was sitting at the machine.

'I'll knock the stuff out myself,' Hood said.

Guardi made a sign and the young man withdrew. As Hood sat down to the keyboard, the machine started up with: GA (the international sign for Go Ahead) IS MR HOOD THERE? WE ARE READY CLAYMORE XXX.

Hood typed: GOOD MORNING. I'M SURE OUR PARTY IS HERE. I WANT YOU TO SEND OUT THE OTHER GIRL WITH WHITNEY AND TWO OF SHAKESPEARE'S MEN.

He sat back. He lit a cigarette and hissed the smoke out. He waited. The machine clicked again. THAT IS IMPOSSIBLE. THE RISK OF LOSING BOTH IS TOO GREAT. THERE ARE OTHER METHODS.

Hood typed back: YOU NAME 'EM. Silence. Hood sent: WELL? Still silence. He typed: IS SHAKESPEARE THERE?

The machine answered: YES HE IS BESIDE ME.

Hood sent: OUR PARTY IS ON THE POINT OF CRACKING THE SYSTEM. MUST ACT UTMOST SPEED. ONLY HOPE IS TO USE SISTER AS BAIT.

Claymore answered: I WILL NOT HEAR OF IT.

Hood sent: THEN YOU CAN GET SOMEBODY ELSE. I'M OUT.

A pause. I HARDLY CONSIDER THAT A WORTHY RESPONSE.

Hood typed: DON'T BE SO BLOODY PONDEROUS.

There was another pause, longer. Then Claymore answered: THERE IS TOO MUCH AT STAKE IT CANNOT XXX VYKS YNSO the message broke off. 'The hell with them,' Hood said.

This time there was a long wait. Hood dragged on his cigarette. Guardi was eyeing him nervously. On the machine, Claymore sent: WAIT.

Hood pictured the scene in the London office with Conder fighting it out with Claymore. He knew what was happening. Conder would understand that Hood would never ask this unless it were vital, the only hope they had.

The machine typed out: I REGRET I CANNOT AGREE. YOU MUST PROCEED OTHERWISE.

Coldly furious, Hood answered: DO YOU THINK THIS IS ROSES? He hoped it sounded belligerent. Nothing came back. The minutes seemed interminable. Hood finished his cigarette, killed it savagely, visualizing Claymore's huge anger. This looked like a bad break-up of the whole enterprise. He punched the keys hard: OK, IT'S A BUST. TOO BAD JACK.

He nodded to Guardi. 'Thanks, that's all. Burn that tape.' He was at the door when the machine clicked into life again. Hood came back, leant forward reading the letters as they spelled out: VERY WELL WE AGREE.

Hood sent back quickly: AGREE WHAT?

WHAT ARRANGEMENTS DO YOU WANT MADE?

That was better. He let 'em sweat. Then he typed: SHE COMES WITH WHITNEY AND TWO SHAKESPEARIANS ONE SPEAKING FLUENT ITALIAN, ALL TRAVELLING STRICTLY AS STRANGERS. GIRL AND WHITNEY GO GRITTI PALACE HOTEL OTHER TWO GRAND HOTEL WHICH NEXT DOOR. NOBODY WILL BE AT AIRPORT REPEAT NOBODY. I WILL CONTACT WHITNEY & OTHERS IN TAVERNA VITTORIA IN CALLE FONTINI WHICH OPENS EARLY & LATE. ESSENTIAL THEY MAKE NO ATTEMPT OTHERWISE CONTACT ME.

He paused. IS THAT CLEAR?

They came back: THAT IS CLEAR. Pause. He could see Claymore's tense furious face. If they didn't like it, they could do something else. He didn't give a damn. Malaren's death had sickened him.

SHAKESPEARE SAYS THEY WILL TAKE THIS AFTERNOON'S PLANE. IS THAT ALL?

Hood sent: NO. ITALIAN SPEAKER IS TO BRING GOOD WORKING KIT. A working kit would enable an extensive variety of disguises for the man to pass himself off as a telephone repair man, postman and so forth.

VERY WELL. ANYTHING MORE?

TELL WHITNEY TO BRING MY COLT. THAT'S ALL.

VERY WELL.

He waited. A long pause. Jerkily the machine said: GOOM-XX GOODLUCK 5+ OLD HWIJ UO#%. Then it was silent.

Hood got up. He tore off the sheet of messages and dropped them into the metal waste-paper basket and threw a match in. Guardi gave a sheepish grin, watching them burn.

'I need three good fast motorboats – fast.'

'We have our own, Mr Hood.'

'I will tell you where I want them. They'd better be good.'

Five minutes later, Hood was outside. He had rung the hotel; but there was still no message from Graff. Hood was puzzled. He did not understand it. His experience of Arthur was that, after this length of time, he would come up with something first-class. In any event, their dangerous game was now set and they must go through with it.

At the Rialto there were the usual crowds. The Japanese were smiling in force. Hood walked on towards the Calle Maggio. Then, in the crowd, he caught sight of the small head and massive shoulders of Henry Moore. Immediately, the man vanished into a doorway. Hood turned. The whippet-faced man he had seen go into the Calle Maggio house with the others was moving out of sight behind a kiosk in the rear. So they had picked him up. They probably had more men out.

His professional reflex yelled at him to get out of the crowd. They could bustle him and drop him dead in seconds with a knife. The water-taxi station by the Rialto was too far back – and the crowd was thicker there. He headed across the small bridge ahead and turned along the Strada Nuova. Then he took a snap decision. He pressed his pace and turned sharp left into the tiny alley alongside the C'a d'Oro, the famous Gothic cinquecento house which was now a museum. He took his ticket at the glass window and went through into the courtyard with its mosaic tiles and pillared portico on the Grand Canal.

He went two steps at a time up the stone staircase to the first floor. At the top he saw Moore and two other beefy bastards, one of them a Negro, pressing at the ticket window. Groups of Japanese were strolling round the great oblong room inside, smiling politely at the walls.

Hood realized he had made a hideous mistake. He had run himself into a trap. The rooms were practically bare and offered nothing in the way of a hiding place; and there were no watchful attendants patrolling the rooms. Stretches of empty red-tinted floor space extended on either side, large areas of bare wall, doorways with no doors. Here and there were a few chairs and long wooden chests against the walls. Left was a tall diamond-paned frosted glass screen and beyond the edge he could see a dozen Japanese standing on the open pillared loggia looking out on the canal.

Hood moved fast towards them and ducked behind the screen. Looks of surprise from the Japanese. They smiled broadly. Hood did not know if Zagora's men had spotted him. He cast around – but there was no retreat from the terrace except through the big room, the way he had come.

Chattering, the Japanese trooped off in a body. Hood sprang to the edge of the loggia, swung one leg over, then the other and took the easy step to the jutting balcony of the adjoining room. For about fifteen seconds he was in full view of the Grand Canal, with his back turned. But there was no alternative.

He stepped through the tall open window into the room. The Japanese raised their heads from the cases of medallions, they turned from smiling at the half-dozen statuettes in the room and smiled at him. One or two bowed. Hood bowed back. There were none of Zagora's men in the room. They had gone for the other side of the house first.

The room where Hood was now was the corner one of the house – and the single door led back into the long bare room he had just quit. Japanese teeth were showing all round. Hood was glad he didn't understand their ping-pong-ball language. He bent earnestly among them at the central table, gazing at the medallions under the glass. But their interest rapidly lapsed and they drifted out. Hood was left alone.

He flattened back against the wall and looked out of the doorway. The big Negro was coming straight along the main room. He had a heavy automatic held close to his side. It was not toy stuff. They were going to blast him and they didn't care if they did it in a museum either.

Hood crouched, grasping one of the long low benches standing along the wall, pressed himself back in readiness and just as the Negro's shadow blocked the light, shot the bench across the doorway like a bolt. It hit the man's shins as he swung in. He toppled forward. His chin had just hit the floor when Hood's kick swung to his head. Hood jumped on the gun wrist and broke that as interest. Then he wrenched the bench back and stepped out of the room.

The stone stair he had come in by was guarded for sure. He knew that at the far end of the long main room there was another internal staircase up and down. He crossed to it and reached the landing – then in one glance, saw Henry Moore and another man on the half-flight down, blocking the exit. Moore spotted him and reached for his gun. Hood jumped up the stairs. Moore was after him fast. At the top, Hood ducked into the first room on the left. No exit. This looked like it.

Henry Moore was at the top stair. Hood pulled his gun. He said under his breath: 'Come in here, Mr Bloody Moore, and I'll make a hole in you.' He did not want to use his gun; it would concentrate them all on him, but what the hell.

Moore charged into the room opposite. Eight paces separated the doors. He heard Moore come out. He raised his gun. Then the man below called out and Moore said: 'What?' and went to the landing. Hood stepped out on tiptoe, crossed silently to the room Moore had just left and flattened against the wall. As he went by, he saw Moore leaning over the banisters talking to the man below. Then Moore turned back and resumed the search, beginning with the room Hood had come from.

Hood let him get away to the front of the building, then stepped out and looked down the stairs. Beefy was standing in the doorway of the main room watching it, back turned. Hood edged down close to the wall, passed behind the man, covering him with his gun in his pocket and reached the turnstile exit below. In the courtyard he hung up for a minute, knowing they were bound to have men in the street. He ran to the portico on the canal. moved out of line of the street door, pulled out his handkerchief and waved it like mad.

Boats chugged by. A girl in one waved back, laughing. Two gondoliers pushed their fares past, staring at him. People came into the courtyard behind. Then a water-taxi did a U-turn and came for him. Hood sat back on the seat. As they turned the big bend in the canal, he looked back. A powerful motor-launch was swinging out from the C'a d'Oro with men in it. He could see five or six.

Hood said to the driver: 'You need a new engine, Mac.'

It was a big polished mahogany launch and it was going to be up with them fast. Hood made the man pull into the next landing-stage, stuffed a fat note into his hand and jumped out. The launch was coming on all right. Hood walked fast over to the small street opposite the pontoon and ran. He turned right and left. He roughly had his bearings. They were going to come up the pontoon and spread.

Then he pulled up short. There was a blocked bridge, under repair – a thing he hardly remembered seeing in Venice before. He had to go back into the area he had just run from to get round. He turned a corner and saw two Negroes coming together along the canal, walking fast. He sprinted back and ran down a side turning. The situation was not good.

Somebody whistled behind him. He sprinted to the corner, swung round it. The next minute he was running across towards the arched doorway opposite – the Palazzo Tomasini, now the antique business of Dick Aldino, an old friend. There was a big courtyard inside strewn with antique statues, stone capitals, well-heads, wrought ironwork, a couple of Reg Butlers, all spread in confusion. Somebody was sawing stone and it made loud screeches.

Hood walked quickly round to the door. Celio, Aldino's stone-mason, looked up from sawing, waved a hand to Hood: 'Buon giorno, signor!' There was an apprentice sawing too. Hood gave Celio a salute and silently pointed upward at the house.

'The padrone is not there,' Celio called out. 'But you know the way. Help yourself, signor.'

Hood nodded and went in. The steep enclosed staircase, with a gilded ceiling *à caissons* – as splendid as any in Venice – led up to vast rooms full of antiques. Dick Aldino was rich, had started as a collector and then gone into the business, though selling was not his interest as much as hunting out fine pieces, lending to museums, living with the things and devoting himself to them. The ruined splendour of the Palazzo Tomasini was a tremendous cadre for all this and Aldino had fixed up old draperies, hangings and so forth to complete it.

The room was lighted by six tall windows. Hood lit a cigarette and passed down, looking at the objects. In half an hour, he reckoned, it would have cooled off outside. A charming Bernini figure of Venus holding a mirror took his eye. He stood enjoying it. Alongside, was a fifteenth-century alabaster altar-piece.

There was a metallic click behind him. Hood ducked instinctively and swung round. It was Henry Moore and the click had come from a burp gun – a stubby sub-machine-gun like a Sten gun – which he was bringing up to shoot. Hood dropped behind the pedestal, pulled his automatic. Moore held his fire. Suddenly Celio's stone-saw started screeching outside and Hood said quietly: 'Christ!' A few seconds earlier and he wouldn't have heard the click. He would have been a dead pigeon.

He took a quick darting look round the pedestal and

flashed back. Moore fired. There was a shattering crash behind Hood's head, Hood glanced back seeing a gigantic Sevres urn smashed to bits. £4,000! He flinched.

He peered out round the other side of the base. He just had time to see Moore crouching behind a Canova marble and Moore let loose another burst. A five-foot *famille verte* porcelain statue of Kuan Yin crashed. £15,000! Hood muttered silently. Without warning there was a fresh burst and chips flew off the nose of a porphyry Roman bust close at hand – a gorgeous piece – £1,200 (former collection of Duke of Dorset, flashed through Hood's mind).

He gave a grim laugh. But he also wanted urgently to move from his bad cover. He dare not take a look; Celio's screeching saws drowned the sound and he realized that Moore could shift round and get a bead on him without his hearing.

He glanced round. Not a mirror in sight. He stared up at the gigantic Louis XIV chandelier. A movement was reflected in the smooth crystal ball hanging at the bottom. He looked out. Moore was scrambling behind an Oeben commode. Hood dived under cover of Pompadour's dog-kennel, partly protected by a marble Leda, and took a snap shot but instantly realized he had missed. There was a crash, he darted a look and saw a Louis XV Meissen candelabra shivering to pieces.

Moore sprayed a burst. A Byzantine reredos disintegrated. £45,000! Only six of them in the world. Now only five – and all in America!

It was excruciating, horrifying and yet sardonically comic. Hood was laughing grimly. Moore was crawling. Hood caught a movement among some Maximilian suits of armour, glimpsed a hand – and snapped off a shot again. Another miss; but it was close enough to make Moore shift cover once more. Moore fired from the hip, brought down a big gilt-framed Uccello portrait above Hood, which toppled on a superb Coldion terracotta group (£7,500) and crashed it, bringing down a mother-of-pearl *nécessaire* (Bauché 1810; £15,000).

Hood struggled, partly buried, seeing Moore running through a grove of settees and chairs, seeking better cover. Hood tried a hard one – and winced as the bullet ricocheted off a Leleu gueridon – but it made Moore scramble faster. He ducked into the adjoining room. Groaning with suppressed laughter, Hood followed.

The room was still bigger. Moore let fly a volley. A blue Barberini glass vase by Hood's head exploded in a shower. A bargain at £20,000. (£30,450 at Christie's for the Portland Barberini, Hood recalled.)

Shots whistled past his head. A rose-Pompadour soup tureen went up in a fountain of fragments. £10,000! Hood's tight-lipped laughter was coming in bursts. Blinking the tears from his eyes, he tried an outflanking move but a Moore volley blasted a big Andrea della Robbia relief panel alongside, spraying him with £14,000 worth of terracotta chips. There was a moment's silence, then a curse. Hood peeked. Moore was crouching behind a Laocoon. His gun seemed to be giving trouble. Hood could see a half-inch of head protruding. He lifted his gun to shoot. Moore kept moving. The scalp dipped out of view, rose again. Hood thought he might just take it. He shut his lips tight – then saw the grey jade Ming bull of the Emperor Yung Lo just behind Moore's head. It was priceless – unique! A miss and he would hit it. Moore's head rose a tiny fraction. Wincing, Hood took aim. He steadied. But he couldn't do it. He couldn't bring himself!

Moore disappeared and his muzzle came out a foot to the right. Hood ducked quickly back as a tall secretaire (French eighteenth-century, signed BVRB) shattered next to him. £17,000.

Hood was crying silently in his grim joy. He wanted to throw himself down and roll on the floor. Hollow peals shook him as he flattened and took aim underneath a neighbouring table. The shot broke a Charteris sideboard dish (£15,000).

All at once, Moore threw his gun aside, evidently out of ammunition. He was still crouching but offered a good shot at a knee. Hood fired snap, wood splinters flew off and he saw it was a sixteenth-century figure by Tilman Riemanschneider. No more shells.

Hood rammed the gun into his pocket and jumped after Moore. Moore swung round, wielded a silver chamberpot (Charles Liger, 1736; £3,000) and hurled it – and ran for the far room. On the way he snatched a two-handled early Chou vessel and threw it. Oh hell – no! Hood called out mentally, Desperately, he dived, caught it and put it quickly on a table, scrabbled to his feet, picked up a blue and white fourteenth-century potiche jar – then rapidly put it back (other of the pair in the British Museum), reached for a Maestro Giorgio lustre dish and hurled that. Henry Moore was trying to lift a Canova statuette. The dish caught him on the chin. He staggered, reeled back but before Hood could close, his arm swept over an outsize lacquer screen and crashed it in Hood's path.

Hood tripped and went down.

Moore was behind a rampart of black lacquer Louis XV commodes and had found an ammunition dump of Nymphenburg, Kaendler Meissen and jade. A piece of Ming hurtled past Hood's head and broke in fragments on a Thorwaldsen bacchante.

Hood saw his chance. Kneeling he crawled round under cover of Lady Younghusband by Cellini and sprang. He landed on Henry Moore's back. They grappled and rolled. Hood snapped two of Moore's fingers and gave him a mighty elbow jab to the face. But Moore was using his granite head to butt. He broke Hood's neck-lock, twisted and caught Hood a terrific butt under the chin.

The room darkened and swam. Moore gave him another. Hood flopped. Dimly he heard Moore clattering among the surrounding things. He was shaking his head, trying to bring himself to. He had a nose-bleed.

There was an interlude during which he thought he passed out. When he stirred everything was still. He dragged one arm out of a holed canvas: a Canaletto. He got shakily to his feet, moving his sore jaw, hoping for no broken teeth. Moore had vanished. He gazed round at the wreckage. He knew he had to get out before they came back for him.

He shook his head. His nose was caked with blood. A big Directoire glass was lying lopsided and smashed by the wall. He straightened himself out in it and picked his way to the door. Miraculously preserved, was a porcelain figure of a guitar-player in the Capo di Monte style. Hood had always thought it bogus. He gave it a gentle push.

Outside, Celio raised a hand from his sawing. His long white moustache smiled and he sang out: 'Buon giorno, signor!'

Hood rang Giulio from a café, said he wanted to switch his address and could he have the villa? This was Giulio's small house three streets away which Giulio rented to rich Americans in the summer but was empty now. Giulio said of course, he would have Hood's things sent round. The housekeeper and her husband who lived there as a regular thing would look after him. 'Thanks Giulio, you're a pal.'

'There's a message for you here, by the way. They told me you were anxious about one.'

'Who's it from?'

'Wait a minute. I'll send for it.'

Hood lit a cigarette while he waited. He was tense.

It was from Arthur Graff. 'Shall I read it?' Giulio said.

'Go ahead.'

'"Important I see you. Suggest 6 pm at Scotti's. I do not want to hang about so if not there I shall be in San Redentore. In case we miss each other, will leave word with the sacristan. Do not return to Calle Maggio because you have been seen. Arthur."' Giulio finished reading. 'That's all.'

'Sure . . . hang on a minute, Giulio . . .' Hood dragged on his cigarette. He was thinking fast. The name of Scotti's seemed to authenticate it; it was the trattoria near the church which he and Graff used habitually when Hood was in Venice and had somehow missed out this time. 'Send it round to the villa, Giulio, will you?'

'Certainly.'

Hood hung up. He went back into the main room of the café. There were a couple of customers drinking coffee. The place looked fine – cool, clean and darkish. There was the blank stone wall of a church opposite. That was fine too.

He asked if he could have some food and the fat smiling woman said of course. They brought him some *antipasto,* a slice of grilled tunny, crisp bread and a half-carafe of Capramontana. The food was delicious and Hood felt restored by it and the atmosphere. He took his time, smoked a cigarette with his coffee, paid and went out.

His clothes and things had already arrived when he reached the villa. Ida, the housekeeper, greeted him, gave him the keys and an envelope with Giulio's message. Hood read it through again. It was in Arthur's handwriting, all right. Good, then. He folded it and put it in his pocket. Then he rang Guardi at the bank. Guardi said he had arranged for the motorboats and gave him the address and telephone number of the man in charge of them. Hood told him to send the senior man with a boat to be at the Rio San Margherita at 5.40 without fail.

'Certainly, Signor Hood,' Guardi said.

Hood freshened up, carefully checked his gun and loaded it. His neck wound was giving him hell but there was nothing to be done about that yet. He waited until 5.42 then went out. The motorboat was at the appointed place, a good-looking job in the usual polished mahogany with white-covered cushions with blue piping at the edges. The boatman had the Venetian shade of red hair. Hood told him where to go and sat back.

It was a cool windless evening with the sky streaking mauves and greens like one of Bonington's Adriatic seascapes. The sound of bells came across the lagoon as they headed out towards Giudecca. It was peace itself, and

Hood absorbed it all the more gratefully because of the crunch that was coming.

The boat stopped at the pontoon a short distance away from the meeting place and tied up. Hood told the man to wait.

'Stay in the boat; don't leave it. Do you understand?'

'Si, signor.'

It was the hour of dusk which Hood disliked. *Entre chien et loup,* the French said, which described it all right. Lights were shining across the water, there was a passenger liner at the berth opposite.

Hood walked past San Redentore church to Scotti's. It was empty; too early for the dinner hour and no Arthur drinking wine at a table as Hood had expected. He went through to the back and Signora Scotti greeted him volubly. She had only just returned from a day with her family at Chioggia. Her husband who had been on the premises all the time had undoubtedly seen Arthur, but he had gone across to the main island for some things.

'Never mind,' Hood said. 'I'll stroll down the quay and find him. If he turns up, tell him to wait for me.'

He turned back to the church and went up the steps to the door. There was apparently no Mass tonight. The nave was empty. Hood walked slowly down it. A woman was praying in a side chapel. Arthur didn't seem to be here.

Hood went through the passage into the sacristi; but that was empty too. He would wait a moment to see if the sacristan had the message. Hood stood in the crude electric light looking round at the familiar effigies in their glass jars and the saintly relics. Then he jolted. He had to take a grip on himself. 'Oh my God,' he said quietly under his breath.

Arthur Graff's head was staring from under one of the glass domes. They had killed him, decapitated him and done this. The eyes were open, the lips slightly parted. The flesh looked as if it had been lightly powdered before being placed there. The stand on which the head rested under the glass was inscribed S. Laurentius A

Brund generalis or. c., meant for the painted effigy which they had removed.

Hood turned away. He felt ill. Arthur had known he was getting in too close, finding out too much, poor devil. They had caught him and made him write the note and then . . . . He shuddered. Then he halted and stood in the shadow of a column. The church was dimly lighted. They might also be waiting here for him.

He could see nobody but the woman who was now arranging some flowers in front of an ex voto in the chapel. He walked quietly along the aisle to the door. He stood just inside, in the shadow of the porch scanning the surroundings outside. He could see nothing unusual. Then he noticed the two big Negroes in the doorway of the scrap-dealer's yard on the right.

One was laughing and demonstrating something to the other. Something flashed very briefly once or twice in his hands. It wasn't a knife or a razor. The man let one end go and swung it by the other and Hood got a glimpse – a length of thin wire on two handles, the sort of thing used to cut through cheese.

The Negroes were laughing, both absorbed in their amusement. The first one did a little dance.

The muscles of Hood's neck and shoulders contracted as he fought the impulse to go over and take retribution. But he had no right to risk it. It did not make the cold unemotional sense he was supposed to go by. Tickle and Whitney were already in town. They had to locate Tiara and try to rescue her and nothing must deflect them from that.

'But by God, I'll chalk it up for you,' Hood said with clamped teeth watching the two Negroes. He transferred his gun to his outer pocket, turned up his coat collar and stepped out. He crossed quietly to the left-hand balustrade of the steps and dropped over. Opposite was a door. He went through into the church-school playground. A Capucin father was crossing at the far end. Hood waited until he had gone, then went through and found a further door which gave on to an alley. In a few moments, he had reached the quay.

Hood went quickly back to the boat and got in. By now Whitney and the others were waiting at the rendezvous. He told the man to cross to the entrance of the Grand Canal.

CHAPTER TWELVE

WHITNEY AND two other men were sitting in the back room of the Taverna Vittoria pretending to drink wine. Outside, the main salle was busy and full of noisy talkers. Hood exchanged brief greetings. With Whitney, Conder had sent Dick Flower, a chinny young man and Ed Page, short and dark, who turned out to be the Italian speaker; he was bilingual. They had all reached the tavern separately.

'The girl in?' Hood said when the waiter had served him with a Scotch.

Whitney nodded. 'In her room at the Gritti. Orders not to leave it on any account.'

'Good.'

'What's this?' Whitney said, indicating the dressing on Hood's neck wound.

'Somebody bit me.'

'I had a girl like that once.'

'Was that the algebra teacher?'

'Yeah. How d'you know?'

' "A" plus "b",' Hood said.

'Yeah!'

'Now this is the job,' Hood said. 'We're going to sit her out on that floating pontoon terrace the Gritti has on the Grand Canal. It's the smartest place in Venice and easily the most eye-catching. Every boat in Venice goes by. If you want to be seen, that's where you are seen. The smart end of Florian's isn't nearly so good and we can't watch her in Harry's Bar without being spotted.

'They are bound to see her there pretty fast. Zagora's been trying to get Tiara, her sister, to make some mental communication with her, to call her out here – I won't go into how, it's pretty complex (he was addressing Flower and Page) but Chuck here understands it. So we put Tickle out there on that terrace as if she has responded, as if she has got this message from her sister and come out in answer to it. She's bound to look a bit uneasy, which will exactly fit the bill; it's the sort of state she would be in naturally.

'When they've sighted her they'll move in and try to collect her. They won't want to wait – and I'm hoping they won't want to give too much study to the surroundings because they'll be too anxious about other people, including me, running into the girl.

'What we have to do is to be waiting when they come for her or send for her.'

Whitney said: 'Can I butt in a minute, Charles? I'm maybe thick-headed tonight but there's something I don't see. Okay, we jump in when they come for Tickle. But how is this going to help us locate Tiara? They're probably holding Tiara fifty miles out of town. Why shouldn't they be?'

Hood said: 'Because they're not going to get the girl moving unless she gets sight or sound of her sister. Since they've got Tiara anyway, they are going to use her to pull her sister into the bag. Tickle's already been scared with that kidnap attempt in London. She's supposed to have slipped away as it is. And if none of this holds, Zagora has got to have the two girls together eventually, so Tickle is bound to lead us to Tiara. If we have to chase fifty miles – hell, we have to chase fifty miles.'

'Okay.'

Hood went over the arrangements and they discussed them carefully.

Hood and Whitney would take up position in one of the small dead-end inlets off the opposite side of the Grand Canal, probably the one alongside the Palazzo Dario. The other two would be stationed in the street alongside the Gritti where there was a convenient café. One of the three motorboats Guardi had supplied would stand by to take Tickle wherever she had to go. Hood and Whitney would use another and Flower and Page the third.

'Best to split up, not all sink or swim together.' With Tickle installed on the terrace, they would keep out of sight watching. She would find some way of indicating where she was going, probably by dropping a note.

In the meantime, Page would take a look at the house in the Calle Maggio. He would choose a get-up from the kit and use some pretext to get in, posing as an Italian, and snoop. Failing that, he could probably learn something from the café or the neighbours. He could report to Hood by phone later. In any event, they would take up position, with Tickle on the terrace, at ten o'clock tomorrow morning.

'All straight?' Hood looked round their faces.

They all nodded.

'Then let's go. Quit separately.'

A clock struck the half-hour. Hood looked at his watch again. Half past three.

'God Almighty.' They had been watching and waiting since ten. The tension was becoming unbearable.

At eleven o'clock, he had glimpsed one of Zagora's men on a passing water-taxi, but since then, nothing had happened. He looked across at Tickle. She was sitting, beautiful, patient and alone, on the floating terrace which gave on to the Gritti bar. She had sat there since morning. She had lunched there among half a dozen other guests; but none of them had approached her.

Hood lit another cigarette. He had black fear that the plan wasn't going to work. Zagora might already have broken Tiara down. Claymore was right – they were taking a purely gratuitous risk and probably facing defeat. Yet what else now was there to do? Page had gone scouting to the Calle Maggio last night and reported back puzzled within an hour, saying: 'Have I got the address right? 3712A Calle Maggio?'

'That's right.'

'The place is an art gallery. Bunch of young Italians just hanging the show. They're genuine all right. No sign of anybody else.'

So that was that. It was obvious from the note they had made Arthur Graff write before they murdered him that they had spotted Hood hanging round the Calle Maggio and skipped.

His attention snapped taut. A hotel bell-boy had come out, gone across to Tickle's table and said something. Tickle got up.

'Here we go,' Whitney said.

Tickle went inside through the glass-panelled door to the bar and turned as if she were going to the telephone box. Hood watched tensely. Flower and Page would signal any landward move. But would they have time, would she do exactly as she had been told? Above all, would Zagora pull some trick at the last moment?

The minutes went by. There was no sign of her, no signal from Flower or Page. She had disappeared inside the hotel.

'She's left her gloves and things on the table,' Whitney said. That was as arranged. If the call were from Tiara she would come back on to the terrace again, pick them up and leave a scribbled word in their place which Page would quickly retrieve so that they could pursue.

Still no Tickle.

'Christ, what's gone wrong?' Hood said.

'I don't like this much, Charles.'

'I hate it, boy.'

Then Tickle came out. It was difficult to see her expression at this distance, but her manner seemed a little nervous. She walked to her chair and table, picked up her gloves, sunglasses, magazine. There was a casual movement which could have been her leaving the note. Then she turned and spoke to the porter behind her.

'Did she leave it?' Hood said.

'I think she put it on the chair,' Whitney said.

The next minute, Hood said: 'What the hell – that's not our boat!' Tickle had evidently asked him to call her boat, the porter had turned looking for one, and a boat had surged out from the small canal alongside the Gritti and swung to the terrace. Tickle got in.

'Doesn't she know that's not our boat?'

'We didn't show her the boatmen.'

The mistake – the fatal mistake had been made! The boat was pulling away fast and Whitney was yelling to their boatman to cast off. 'Let's go after them – quick there!'

'For God's sake hold it!' Hood said. 'If we go charging out there, the game's up. We've got to hold back.' He signalled to the boatman to cast off and keep her idling.

Still in cover, they saw Page dart out on to the Gritti terrace towards the chair Tickle had left. The porter had just picked up the note and looked at it. Page was at his side in a bound. Then with amazement, Hood and Whitney saw an argument start up – an argument at this, of all moments! The porter, for some reason, would not give up the note – no doubt ethical and all to be praised; but unforeseen! He was becoming excited. Hood cursed. They would have a fight on their hands next. The launch with Tickle was drawing farther away every moment up the Grand Canal.

'Get down!' Hood pressed Whitney down in the boat with him and shouted to the boatman to pull over to the Gritti. At that moment, above the gunwale, he saw Page grip the porter's arm, open the man's hand with a nerve-jab and snatch the note.

The porter shouted and swung for him. Flower and his boat were alongside, Page jumped in and they stood off. As Hood's boat came up, Page yelled: 'Athena Buberheim's. Beauty Care.'

'Okay!' Hood yelled back.

Of course! The Buberheim Institute was the super-swagger home-from-home of half the chic women of Europe and America, enormously costly and supremely elegant – the sort of sphere which Zagora would move in naturally. Athena Buberheim had just opened a new wing in the old Palazzo Tosti where these women fought to get the favour of treatment. It contained, Signora Buberheim had announced, among other things an authentic Byzantine bath, the only one in the world with genuine Byzantine decor. The thing had recently been inaugurated by a Minister.

Page and Flower headed off up the Grand Canal with Hood still crouched in the other boat, following.

'Can you see her, Chuck?'

'Yes – just.'

The launch with Tickle was moving at good speed. Hood realized that Guardi had done an efficient job. Their boats were fast. But the episode over the note had given the launch too big a start.

Hood's jaw muscles were knotted. She was going ... They were going to lose her. He could see the launch far ahead, turning to go down a side canal. Then suddenly it cut speed and came to a stop. Hood couldn't see what had happened; then he wanted to cheer. A big motor job-barge – the sort of craft that delivered coal – was slewing round across the entrance to the side canal. The launch was having to wait while it completed the manoeuvre.

The distance dwindled. Flower and Page cut speed so as not to crowd too close. Hood told his boatman to throttle down. They could see Tickle sitting back, legs crossed. A few moments later, the coal barge had cleared a passage and they moved ahead. Flower and Page were nonchalantly lounging, smoking and chatting, occasionally laughing as if they were a thousand miles from doing what they were doing. In their boat, Hood and Whitney lay flat.

Tickle's launch pulled up at the water-gate of the Palazzo Tosti. The other boats checked and made to stop at a house astern. They saw Tickle get out and go up the steps. The launch pulled away and disappeared.

Whitney stared at Hood. Hood looked back, said nothing. A minute passed – two – three. Whitney's look was scared. He waited a few seconds more, then said: 'For

God's sake, what's the matter? We've got to get in there!'

Hood said through clenched teeth: 'We have to give her time to get in, Chuck.'

'Do you mean to —'

'If we rush in too soon, they'll see we're using her as bait, they'll keep Tiara out of her sight and they'll keep her away for good. We'll never get near her. It'll be all over.'

'If they hustle her out the back —'

'If it were a push-over and there weren't any chances to take, they wouldn't have got this far!'

As the minutes went by, Hood caught anxious looks back from Flower and Page in the other boat. Then he said: 'Time enough. Come on, let's get in there.'

The boats surged forward, they sprang out and ran up the imposing steps. Hood called out: 'Page at the door, Flower upstairs, Chuck through to the back' – and they crowded in.

The entrance was a great oval salon, with high ceiling. There were marble columns, gilt, Savonnerie carpet, an immense antique mirror. It looked like a public building. A woman in black at a marble desk was talking to two strawberry blondes in pastel overalls. On the far side was a nominal male with dyed hair, made-up eyes and willowy hands presiding at a marble counter of ties and scents labelled 'Brine', 'He-Man', 'Rough-Neck', 'Tattoo' and 'Bully'.

Hood and the others went forward among the scent-soap-cream and bath-salts smells. The women stared, immediately hostile. The homo sat up.

'Where's Lady Tiara Evenly?' Hood said. 'And her sister?'

'Lady who?' The woman in black glanced perfunctorily at her book. 'Not here. You've made a mistake.'

'Don't do that!' Hood knocked a bell-push away from her hand. Whitney was heading for the high draped doorway, big enough for a bus, opposite.

'But what are you doing?' She was on her feet, trying to stop him. 'Who — ? You cannot go – how dare you!

Gino! Gino!' The homo minced up, chucking his tongue. 'Tck – oh, have you an appointt-mentt?'

Flower pushed him in the chest and sprang towards the stairs. Quickly Hood went through the doorway, leaving Page to deal with them. Whitney had disappeared. There was a broad passage with girls coming and going between the rows of curtained booths. Another ambiguous creature in trousers and turquoise blouse crossed ahead. Somewhere a woman's high voice was saying: 'Jamais! Jamais! Jamais!'

Hood flipped back the curtain of the first booth. A husky masseuse with a blonde Swedish face was pounding pounds of flesh on a white-covered table. It wasn't Tiara or Tickle. The girl took no notice of him, flipped the customer over and dug in again, wrist-deep.

Hood brushed past the turquoise homo, wrenched back the next curtain – the booth was empty. Next door, a girl swathed in towels lay still with eyes shut on a chaise longue. She shifted and the towel fell, showing all. Not Tiara either.

He could hear the women and the he-man scent specialist kicking up a row in the front salon. Page had his hands full; but he knew what to do. There were muffled thuds from the floor above. Hood flung into the next booth; the masseuse was alone – and the last booth was empty.

The corridor led off. He glimpsed other rooms, a telephone switchboard, showcases, a sign Boutique. Chuck Whitney was down there somewhere. Hood turned and raced back. He ignored the lift and sprang up the monumental staircase. His feet slid on the marble steps. There were gigantic framed pictures on the gilded walls, the pervasive smell of cosmetics. He bumped into a suggestive Leda.

A hipless floor receptionist and an older woman were standing at a desk, obviously aware that something was up. Hood ignored them, getting his bearings. A carpeted corridor with doors all along ran off one way. A sign at a draped arch said 'Coiffure'; another 'Oxygen-relax'.

Another 'Electro-Therapy'. He took the coiffure first. The women under the driers looked up startled over their magazines. Faces turned; combs hung in mid-air. A Pekinese was being curled. But no twins.

As Hood swung back into the corridor, Chuck Whitney came up the stairs. 'No sign down there.'

'Manager?'

Whitney shook his head. 'Office empty.'

Hood gritted his teeth. 'Come on.' They flung open the first door. The hovering receptionist screamed.

The room was big and steamy. There was a girl in a sunken bath full of mud, her head resting back, face covered with a mud-pack. She didn't move. Whitney held back the receptionist and the other woman. Hood advanced, bent over the girl in the bath, looking closely at her face. He extended a hand and scraped off a swathe of wet mud. There was a flutter under the cotton-wool eye-pads, one dropped. A solitary blue eye looked up at him.

'Sorry,' Hood said. 'Not you.'

Her mouth opened pink in the mud-mask and screamed.

The receptionist was tugging at Whitney's arm, protesting. They slammed the door after them and dashed into the next room. The girl on the couch was covered with cream and nothing else. There was a mask of cream and gauze on her face. The assistant paring the girl's toenails stared at Hood. He stepped up, lifted the gauze, wiped a swathe of cream from her face. The eye-pads wobbled again. The girl blinked with cream in her eyes. The magnificent torso moved, cream slithered down the curves. Nipples ogled him. Not Tiara. Hood flung out. The next cubicle was empty.

Hood felt he wanted to break the joint apart. The commotion going on behind them was rising in pitch and he could hear running steps on the floor above.

'Quick!' They swung from one room to the next. In three more there were women under mud-packs. A massive woman with dyed hair, one of the senior staff, had joined the receptionist, scandalized, protesting and trying to stop them.

A recessed door said 'Le Jet'. As Hood turned the handle, the hard beat of water came from the other side. He looked in. It was a big tiled room. A lovely tall naked girl, covered with cream was standing against the far wall waiting to have the cream hosed off her. 'Oh,' she cried in an English voice, crooking coyly a knee. Hood snatched up the hose which was gurgling mildly on the floor at his feet, turned it full on and sprayed her. She put up her hands protectively, turning one way and the other to escape. He moved in closer. It was like slowly stripping her. The cream slithered off her shoulders, bosom, belly, haunches and her long legs. She had a magnificent figure – like Tiara. Damn it! He dropped the hose, stepped up and wiped cream off her face. No luck. It wasn't her.

He slammed the door, burst into the last room. It was empty.

Whitney was facing seven or eight of them now, all vociferating in the corridor. Other girls were hurriedly passing in and out of the rooms. Somewhere a phone was ringing and buzzers going.

He stood there, not knowing what next. Flower came pounding down the corridor. He shouted: 'Not up there.'

'Get back on the stairs!'

An arrow pointed 'Le Bain Byzantine'.

'Chuck!' There was the biggest door Hood had seen outside Versailles. The three women attendants outside screamed as Hood charged in and ran across the big anteroom – more marble and mirrors – lined with clothes closets. A sign by the door on the far side said 'TEPIDARIUM'.

Inside, they pulled up short. It was a big circular domed room in authentic Roman bath style with mosaic flooring. Thirty women were lying on white-covered divans in wrappers, slips or nothing, smoking or reading, or moving round in towels with drinks in their hands, talking, playing cards, phoning among piles of magazines and boxes of sweets. Hood and Whitney took in the costly bosoms and expensive abdomens. Thighs glimpsed only by multi-millionaires were there, some of the most prohibitive generating areas in the Old World and the New.

There were screams. Bare bosoms were covered and some were not. Hood ran among them, pushing aside here and there. But no Tiara or Tickle.

He swung round. 'CALIDARIUM', said the door on the left. They ran into the steamy heat of another circular room. The heat hit Hood like instant tropics. Half a dozen girls and two fat women were lying naked and glistening. Heads were raised. No twins. There were cubicles along one side.

'Take the cubicles, Chuck!'

Hood raced out, across the Tepidarium, now in a furore, and under the sign on the far side 'FRIGIDARIUM' into the adjoining and last room.

There was a round pool, still and icy-looking. Three gorgeous brunettes floated, belly up. They didn't hear Hood come in and he inspected them. But no Tiara.

Hood stood stock still. He was shattered. They had got away with it. He could see some cubicles under the arches on the other side of the pool. He raced round, wrenched them open one after the other, smashing the doors wide – all empty.

In despair he swung round and saw a condemned handle-less door in the corner. He sprang over, charged it. The door shook. The girls in the pool had heard and were splashing out. Whitney came running in on the other side of the pool.

'No luck.'

'Over here!'

Together they got their shoulders to the door – and as it gave, pitched in and nearly fell over Tiara bent over Tickle on the floor.

'Charles! Is it – oh, my God!' She was in his arms.

'What's happened to Tickle?' Tiara was wrapped in a

white towel, as if she had been in the bath; Tickle was still in her street dress, lying unconscious on the floor.

'They gave her a shot of something. They threw us in here a few minutes ago.'

'Who's "they"?'

'The woman who runs this place. She's under Zagora's thumb. They all are here. He operates a lot from here.'

Hood had pulled up Tickle's eyelid. 'Sure. Drugged her. Another few minutes, kid, and they'd have shipped you both out of here. Now *we* are going to ship you both out fast and you're going without uniform, too – in that!'

Whitney picked up Tickle and threw her over his back in a fireman's carry and went for the door.

Suddenly Tiara began to laugh.

Hood looked at her, amused, sagging with relief. Then the laughter became forced and unnatural. It racked Tiara's beautiful body. She threw her head back but could not control it, then her hands came up and clutched her throat as if the laughter were giving her pain.

Hood could not move. He stood there appalled. His mind would not work. Then some impulse made him lift his hand and slap her face twice.

Sharply she drew her breath in. The laughter stopped. She stood looking at him, panting a little, recovering. Then she was close to him with her arms round him.

'Tiara, you had me scared. Now come on and we'll clear the hell out of here.'

They hurried out and across the big domed room adjoining. At the door she checked him. 'Charles – a Tepidarium – it's one of my places; you don't often get the chance.'

'Sure, I have one waiting with tiger-skin rugs.'

GAVIN LYALL

'A complete master of
the suspense technique'
Liverpool Daily Post

SHOOTING SCRIPT
5/-

'The sky's the limit for this
fine suspense/adventure story'
Daily Mirror

MIDNIGHT PLUS ONE
5/-

'Grimly exciting . . . original
in concept, expertly written
and absolutely hair-raising'
New York Times

THE WRONG SIDE OF THE SKY
5/-

'One of the year's best
thrillers'
Daily Herald

'Thrillers on this level
are rare enough'
The Daily Telegraph